# FEMALE TROUBLE

Bolt saw the nickel-plated pistol bouncing around as the dazed woman clutched it in her quivering hand.

"Don't shoot, lady. There's been some mistake," Bolt said as he saw her finger tighten around the trigger. He didn't move a single muscle. He didn't even blink.

"I am going to kill you." There was a sudden eerie husk to her voice.

A chill went down his spine when the woman suddenly lunged toward him, her vacant eyes staring into his. The pistol was no more than five feet from his head and it was aimed right between his eyes.

# BOLT

## An Adult Western Series by Cort Martin

#10: BAWDY HOUSE SHOWDOWN      (1176, $2.25)

#11: THE LAST BORDELLO      (1224, $2.25)

#13: MONTANA MISTRESS      (1316, $2.25)

#15: BORDELLO BACKSHOOTER      (1411, $2.25)

#17: LONE-STAR STUD      (1632, $2.25)

#18: QUEEN OF HEARTS      (1726, $2.25)

#19: PALOMINO STUD      (1815, $2.25)

#20: SIX-GUNS AND SILK      (1866, $2.25)

#21: DEADLY WITHDRAWAL      (1956, $2.25)

#22: CLIMAX MOUNTAIN      (2024, $2.25)

#23: HOOK OR CROOK      (2123, $2.50)

#24: RAWHIDE JEZEBEL      (2196, $2.50)

*Available wherever paperbacks are sold, or order direct from the Publisher. Send cover price plus 50¢ per copy for mailing and handling to Zebra Books, Dept. 2196, 475 Park Avenue South, New York, N.Y. 10016. Residents of New York, New Jersey and Pennsylvania must include sales tax. DO NOT SEND CASH.*

# BOLT
#84

### RAWHIDE JEZEBEL

BY
CORT MARTIN

**ZEBRA BOOKS**
**KENSINGTON PUBLISHING CORP.**

ZEBRA BOOKS

are published by

Kensington Publishing Corp.
475 Park Avenue South
New York, NY 10016

First printing: October 1987

Printed in the United States of America

# CHAPTER ONE

The crack of the rifle shot disturbed what started out as a peaceful afternoon. Bolt twisted in the saddle, clawed for his rifle. But there was no rifle in his scabbard. He heard the low angry whine of the bullet as it passed a foot from his ear, plowed a furrow in the earth some fifty yards beyond. Tom Penrod ducked instinctively, and let out a surprised curse.

"What the hell?" Tom growled. "Some sonofabitch is tryin' to bushwhack us." He stretched his neck and peered out across the tree-studded land.

"Stay down," Bolt warned, drawing his pistol. He looked in the direction of where the shot had sounded and saw the silhouette of a lone rider breaking the horizon.

The two men were out for a Sunday ride, stretching their horses' legs. They were riding across the open back forty of their Rocking Bar Ranch, which was in Cow Town, two miles south of San Antonio. Beyond Cow Town, the rugged prairielands of southern Texas stretched out for long, dusty miles.

Bolt and Tom, childhood friends who had lived the free-spirited life of cattle drovers before they bought the Rocking Bar Ranch, had just ridden across their unmarked property line and onto their neighbor's land. There weren't any fences to separate the two ranches. They didn't need fences. They were friends with their neighbor and the cattle they owned were free to roam the open prairie, although the animals seldom wandered out to the back forty.

They weren't looking for trouble, weren't expecting any. But here it was, riding straight toward them.

"I didn't bring my rifle," said Tom as he edged his horse toward the cover of a cottonwood and drew his pistol.

"Neither did I, dammit," replied Bolt. "I thought we might run across a rattlesnake or a jackrabbit, but not this."

Tom shaded his eyes against the afternoon sun off to his left and waited to get a better look at the oncoming rider. "Drill him when he gets closer, the dirty bastard," he said out of the corner of his mouth. "I don't know who that fool bushwhacker is, but it sure as hell ain't Lem Campbell. Lem wouldn't draw down on us."

"No, it ain't Campbell. Lem's as big as an ox, twice as big as that puny little, rifle-totin' jackass." Bolt squinted his eyes, trying to make out the features of the distant rider, who was barreling toward them like an army scout with an urgent message. He ducked his head instinctively when he saw the rifle aimed his way, just before a second shot cracked the air.

"Jeez!" Tom muttered as he hunched his tall, lanky frame down in the saddle. "What in the hell did we do to bring that fellow's wrath down on us? The dirty sonofabitch!" His lips tightened as he raised his Colt .45, sighted in on the intruder, and waited for the rider to come within pistol range.

"No. Don't shoot, Tom," Bolt called as the rider came closer. "That ain't a feller. That's some damned fool woman shootin' at us."

"Well, I'll be hog-tied. It is a woman." Tom sucked in a deep breath, let it out slowly, then took careful aim at the intruder. "Well, it don't make no difference to me. If the goldarned wench wants to use us for target practice, then she can damned well expect us to return the favor."

"Wait, Tom. She's lowered her rifle. Maybe she's just trying to scare us off."

"Well, she's doing a damned good job of it. Why in the hell would she want to shoot us? We didn't do nothin' to her."

"Maybe we startled her."

"What the hell is she doing riding way out here, anyway?" Tom grumbled.

"Maybe the same thing we're doing, Tom, drinking in the beauty of the land. Riding out across the peaceful countryside on a quiet Sunday afternoon."

"Peaceful? Quiet?" Tom snorted.

"I reckon she's a friend of Lem's." Bolt could tell

by the way the woman rode that she was confident on a horse. He figured that she was just one of a long string of girlfriends whom Lem Campbell brought out to his house. Not that Lem was a lecherous old man. He was a bachelor with simple needs, like having someone to clean his house and cook for him, a woman to take to his bed. Lem swore he'd marry if the right girl came along, but Bolt knew the old man was too set in his ways to ever make the commitment to marriage.

"Then he's got a damned spitfire on his hands this time." Tom shook his head. "I'll bet she's wild in bed, but I wouldn't want to get close enough to that one to find out."

"I didn't think you were that particular, Tom," Bolt chided. "I thought you'd climb the bones of anyone who wore skirts."

Tom glanced at his friend. "Not that gal. She'd probably shoot my balls off when she was through with me."

The hoofbeats pounded the ground as the horse and rider sped toward them. Bolt saw the outline of the woman's long, brown skirt that draped over the animal's flanks. The horse was almost the same color as the woman's dress, maybe a shade darker. The rider's bright red hair jutted out beneath a large, floppy hat, and flowed in the afternoon breeze as she clutched the reins in one hand and held the rifle across her lap with the other.

"She's a pretty young thing, ain't she?" Bolt grinned as the rider came closer. He sat tall in the saddle, his pistol steady in the hand that rested on his leg. He was ready to shoot if he had to.

"How can you say that about some fool gal who's taking pot shots at us?" Tom said.

Bolt's grin faded as the woman rider reined her horse to a quick stop some twenty feet away and raised her rifle again.

"Get off my land!" the red-haired woman shouted. She held the rifle as if it were second nature to her to have the heavy Winchester in her hands, the finger of her right hand poised around the trigger, her other hand cupped under the wooden plate to steady the long barrel. She looked down the length of the barrel at Bolt.

"What do you mean, your land?" Bolt called back. "This land belongs to Lem Campbell and we've got his permission to ride it. Same as we let him ride across our property when he's of a mind to."

"It doesn't belong to Mister Campbell any more," the woman said as she urged her horse closer to the two men with a nudge of her knee to the animal's side. "I own this land now and you're trespassing. Now git!" She motioned with a wave of her rifle.

"Since when?" Tom asked as he squared his shoulders. He held his pistol at his side, pointed it at the ground.

"Since I bought it from Mister Campbell three days ago. Now, get off my land right now or your bones'll become a permanent part of it," the woman said, her voice harsh and oddly deep for her diminutive size. "And I'm warning you, I'm a crack shot."

9

Bolt believed her. The gal was short and appeared to be fragile in her femininity, but he saw the hard, cold flash of determination in her glaring green eyes.

"We didn't know that Lem had sold out," he said politely as he slid his pistol into its holster. "You can put your rifle away, ma'am. We'll be ridin' on back to our own property."

"Don't ma'am me," she snapped. "And I'll be puttin' my rifle away when you two boorish louts are gone."

The breeze flapped at the delicate yellow scarf the woman wore around her neck, and ruffled her long, red hair. The same early-summer breeze carried the heady scent of her perfume to Bolt's nostrils. He breathed in the flowery fragrance and studied her tightly pursed lips, which were ruby red with the lipstick she wore. He saw the round blotches of rouge on her cheeks, the powder on her face that made her look like a delicate, painted, china doll. He guessed her to be in her late twenties, a couple of years older than he and Tom were. He figured she'd lived a rough life, judging from the way she handled the rifle. He noticed the harsh lines in her face, the dark circles under her eyes where there wasn't enough face powder to hide them.

A sudden flush of discomfort settled in Bolt's chest when he realized he was staring at the pretty woman, mesmerized by her haughty beauty, thrown off balance by her delicate fragrance. She didn't fit his image of a rough-and-tumble gun-totin' female.

10

He shifted position in his saddle and dropped his gaze to the ground for a moment, but couldn't keep his eyes off her. He noticed the proud way she sat her horse and wondered who she was. He glanced down at the long rifle in her small, steady hands, then looked up into her glaring eyes. He smiled at the woman and hoped he wasn't pushing his luck.

"Sorry," he said lamely. "We'll be leaving now."

"Hmph," the redhead snorted.

"Where are you from, miss?" Tom asked as he holstered his pistol.

"I have no time for idle talk," the woman said. She shot Tom a dirty look and swung the heavy rifle in his direction.

Tom shrugged his shoulders. "Excuse me, ma'am. Just thought I'd ask."

"I'm from Dodge City, if it really matters to you," she said. "Now git. Both of you. Before I blow your bulbs off." She lowered the rifle slightly, aimed it at Tom's crotch.

Tom winced, glanced at Bolt.

Bolt couldn't help but smile. "I reckon you were right, Tom."

"About what?" the woman asked, turning toward Bolt as she relaxed her grip on the rifle.

"Nothing, ma'am."

"I said not to call me . . ."

Bolt saw her tense, saw the rifle come up into position again. "Sorry," he said. "It's considered polite where I come from."

"Then that's your problem, mister, and I really don't give a damn. The only thing I care about is

11

that you and your friend get off my property right now and that you stay off."

Bolt couldn't understand the woman's hostility toward them. The strangers he'd come across over the years were usually friendly, at least at first meeting. Hell, even the hardened outlaws nodded or tipped their hats when passing on the open trail. But this gal had come at them, rifle blazing. They'd done nothing to deserve her vicious attack, and yet she'd fired at them without even bothering to find out who they were. His curiosity got the best of him.

"Look, lady, as long as we're going to be neighbors, I reckon we ought to introduce ourselves," he said. "My name's Bolt and this is my partner, Tom Penrod." He nodded and gave her a slight tip of the hat, a gesture that was so natural to him, he wasn't even aware that he'd done it.

"I know who you are," she said without blinking an eye.

Bolt saw the sparks of hatred flash in her eyes, saw her clench her teeth tight. So that was it, he thought. Lem Campbell had told her about the bordello he and Tom ran on their ranch. Well, that wasn't his worry. She was the one who had chosen to move in next door to them, and she'd just have to take what came with the territory. He wasn't about to shut down his whorehouse just to please this arrogant, holier-than-thou bitch.

"Yeah, I guess Lem told you about us," he said.

"He didn't have to, Mr. Bolt," she said coldly. "Your reputation is widespread."

"Oh? I didn't know I had one." He noticed that

12

she lowered the rifle to a resting position on her lap.

"Your Rocking Bar Ranch and Bordello is famous, or infamous, all throughout the West. In fact, I was quite surprised to see that you actually have cattle on your ranch."

"You got a name, lady?"

"It's Jessie Belle," the woman answered, with no warmth to her voice.

"Jezebel?" Tom mocked as he looked her up and down. "It's a fittin' name, ma'am."

"It's Jessie Belle," she barked as she glared at Tom. She threw her shoulders back, sat taller in the saddle and looked at Bolt again. "I tell you my name for your information only, certainly not to be neighborly."

"Can't we at least be pleasant to each other, under the circumstances?" Bolt said.

"I hardly think so," Jessie said. "You see, we're going to be competitors and I don't think there's any room for friendliness between us."

"Oh? Well, there's plenty of land for cattle to graze around here and there's always a demand for the beef we raise, so I don't think there'll be much competition between us."

"That's not what I meant," she said with an arrogant toss of her head. "I'm not going to mess with cattle."

"Then what in the hell do you mean?" Bolt said, not caring if his impatience showed. "Say it straight, woman."

The redhead smiled for the first time, but it was a smug smile that didn't show any teeth. "I'm

13

going to open my own bordello. The Proud Peacock. And believe me, I plan to give you plenty of competition. I'm surprised you haven't heard about it."

"We've got better things to do than to keep track of the comings and goings of our neighbors." Bolt stared dumbly at her, unable to believe his ears. No, he hadn't heard about the new bordello. He hadn't been to town in almost a week and wouldn't ride to San Antonio again until the next day when he would take the buckboard in for supplies. Somehow, he just couldn't imagine this small, dainty woman running a whorehouse or dealing with the rowdy men who would patronize her establishment.

As he studied her more closely, the shock of reality settled in and formed a ball of lead in the pit of his stomach. This Jessie Belle was dead serious, and with the kind of fierce determination she'd already displayed, she could put him out of business.

"You? Running a whorehouse?" Tom laughed. "It appears to me you'd be more the type to be teachin' little children to read and write. That would be a nice, safe profession for you."

Bolt cursed under his breath when he saw the little woman curl her finger around the trigger. Why couldn't Tom just keep his mouth shut?

"Don't make light of it, Mr. Penrod," Jessie said tightly. "I'm sure you and Mr. Bolt will come to loathe me."

"I'm sure we will," Tom retorted.

"I'm opening The Proud Peacock tonight," Jessie said, ignoring Tom, "and since your bordello is closed on Sunday nights, I should do a rip-snortin' business tonight." Her bright red lips curled to a proud, haughty smile, but the expression of hatred lingered in her eyes.

"I wish you luck," Bolt said, swallowing the hard lump in his throat.

"Within a week, I promise you, you'll lose so much business, you'll both be wishing you could find jobs as common cow hands."

"Don't count on it," Bolt said. He tightened his fingers around the reins, tugged them to the right. "Good day, Miss Belle."

"You're both invited to my grand opening tonight," Jessie said, her husky voice tinged with sugary sarcasm. "There'll be free champagne and a fine spread of vittles. It'll give you a chance to see what I'll be offering in the way of competition."

"No thank you," Bolt said.

"Why, Mr. Bolt, you can't bury your head in the sand and pretend we're not there. Besides, I think you'll be surprised by the beautiful, elegant ladies who work for me. They'll put your sluts to shame. In fact, bring your gals along so they can see what class is all about."

"Thanks anyway," Bolt said, "but we'll have to decline your kind invitation. Sunday is a day of rest for us and for our harlots. We won't be bothering you again." He turned away from Jessie Belle and swung his horse around. Tom did the same and urged his horse up alongside Bolt's.

"I hope you'll change your mind about the

party," Jessie called, "but just remember, the only way you'll be welcome on my property from now on is as paying customers at The Proud Peacock."

Bolt glanced over his shoulder at the red-headed woman. "You won't be seein' me, then," he said. "I don't pay to sleep with women."

"Of course not," Jessie laughed haughtily. "Not when you can romp with your own sluts free of charge."

"I don't do that either, ma'am."

"Oh really?" Jessie said, a puzzled look on her face. "I'd think you'd take advantage of your situation. Most men would."

"I don't mix business and pleasure," Bolt said simply. "Goodbye, Miss Belle, and good luck on your new venture."

Bolt turned away from her, snapped the reins. His horse, Nick, started out, heading for home. Tom followed him.

"One more thing, Mr. Bolt," Miss Belle called out.

Again, Bolt swung around in the saddle and looked at the woman with the flowing red hair. The rifle she aimed at him was almost as big as she was. She was so small, it was hard for him to take her threat seriously, but he had no doubt that Jessie Belle would pull the trigger with little provocation.

"Yair?" he said.

"You're much more handsome than I had imagined you would be, Mr. Bolt." With that, she lowered her rifle, reined her horse around, dug her heels into the horse's flanks, and took off at a gallop in the opposite direction.

Puzzled by her blunt remark, Bolt frowned as he watched her ride away from them.

"Well, I'll be damned," he muttered as he swung around in his saddle and rode slowly alongside his friend. "She thinks I'm handsome."

"Don't let it go to your head, Bolt," Tom said. "She's just another pretty face."

"Don't worry, Tom, I don't cotton to a gal like that. Hell, she's so cold, she'd break into little chunks of ice if you tried to mount her."

"I agree," Tom sighed. "So what are you gonna do about her?"

"Nothing. Leave her alone. What's there to do?"

"But you can't let her open the bordello next door to us," Tom protested.

"I can't stop her, Tom."

"You know that every damned feller who rides out here from town will pass by her place first. Hell, she can snag 'em off the trail and we'll never see another customer. That little bitch'll ruin us."

"Then that's a chance we'll have to take. She's got a right to run a business, same as we do."

"Well, it ain't right and you know it," Tom roared. "We were here first and she's gonna cut into our profits. How in hell can you stay so calm about it?"

Bolt glanced over at his friend and smiled.

"Relax, Tom. After all, a little competition ought to be healthy for us."

"Competition, yes. But not downright treacherous destruction by a vicious little bitch like that."

Bolt grinned. "Aw, she's not that bad, Tom."

17

"We'll see," said Tom wryly.

Bolt had no doubt that they would. Jessie Belle, he was sure, was no wilting flower. She would be seen as well as heard from. If she had been a man, he would have said she had balls.

# CHAPTER TWO

Tom Penrod pawed at his food all during supper. He kept talking about The Proud Peacock until Bolt told him to shut up.

"But we really ought to go over there tonight. Hell, we been offered. And we'd be fools not to check out the competition."

"I think we all ought to go over there," said Linda Ramsey, a strawberry-cheeked blonde, who had more than her share of spunk. She and the other girls had been listening to Tom's description of Jessie Belle with more than idle curiosity. "I'd like to see what her girls look like."

"Me too," said Doris Fletcher, a new girl who had drifted in out of the cold of Denver two months before and had established herself as a favorite in Bolt's bordello. She was petite, dusky-skinned, with shining black hair and nut-brown eyes. A comely mole off-centered just above her upper lip. Her nose was aquiline, delicately-shaped, and, with her high round cheekbones, gave her a regal appearance, Grecian or Roman, depending upon the way she combed her hair and banded it with tortoise-shell or ribbon.

Linda Ramsey was sturdier, plainer, but she

exuded an earthy sensuality that stirred the customers to flock to her bed in steady queues from Friday afternoon to Sunday morn. She had cloudy blue eyes that bespoke of forbidden bedrooms and womanly secrets even in the harsh light of day, and her breasts pushed against her bodice like melons bursting to ripen on gentle garden mounds. Her skin was creamy alabaster, all silk and honey and sweet milk, begging men to touch and sip of her nectar. Her smile was broad and natural, her teeth still good because she did not chew or smoke tobacco. She rubbed her teeth with ashes and pumice, freshened her kiss with mint leaves and paid for flowery perfumes out of her own earnings, scents that spoke of exotic ports in far-flung lands: Singapore, Calcutta, Tangiers, or incense-filled boudoirs in San Francisco or Juarez or Matamoros. She was all things to all men, and Bolt often wondered what it would be like to spend a night with her because he saw the glazed look in the men's eyes when they came from her room and staggered away in the darkness, content and speechless.

"I already told the woman we would not be there," said Bolt, with conviction.

"Seems to me it's right unneighborly to refuse," said Tom, for once somewhat diplomatic and arrowing in on a point that Jared couldn't ignore. "I mean we'd look downright unhospitable if we didn't drink some of that fiery lady's champagne."

"Oh, please," said Abby Mason, playing with the velvet choker around her delicate neck. "It

20

would be so exciting to go to a party tonight, and you said Miss Belle invited all of us."

Abby, a fun-loving gal from St. Louis, was one of the girls Lem Campbell had brought home to live with him in his effort to find a suitable wife. She had stayed with the old codger for only a short spell, just long enough to realize that Lem was more interested in having a cook and cleaning lady, and someone to trim his smelly toenails, than he was in having a young, playful bed partner.

"I don't know," said Bolt as he pushed his plate aside and wiped his mouth with a napkin. He saw the same sparkle of eagerness in Abby's hazel eyes that he'd seen the first time he'd met her. Lem had brought her along for a visit one Sunday night and Abbey had spent most of the evening making friends with Bolt's harlots. She had that fresh-scrubbed look of a young maiden just stepping out of her Saturday-night bath, and the light brown ringlets of her naturally curly hair only added to that illusion.

It hadn't been long after that first meeting before Abby had come begging him to take her on as a harlot, so that, as she said, she wouldn't die of boredom. He had been impressed by her enthusiasm, by her joy for life, and had finally been swayed into hiring her because of her playful pleading, after she assured him that she'd already left Lem. He saw that same little-girl begging in her eyes now, as if she were asking to go to a birthday party.

"It—it's so boring here on Sunday nights,"

Abby pleaded, "and we'd really like to go for a ride in the moonlight. We wouldn't have to stay very long. Please, Bolt. . . ."

"You ought to go," urged Harmony Sanchez, the beautiful blond woman who wore many hats at the ranch: madam; house mother for the girls; cook, cleaning lady and sock-darner for Bolt and Tom; and on many occasions, a very willing bed partner for Bolt. A happy-go-lucky gal, she loved everything she did, especially crawling into Bolt's soft featherbed.

"Will you go with us?" Bolt asked.

"No. Visiting a whorehouse is not the way I choose to spend my Sunday evenings," Harmony said, "but the rest of you should go and check out the competition."

"Harmony's right," said Linda Ramsey.

Bolt's lips stretched into a shadowy smile. His eyes flickered with understanding. He looked at Tom, almost laughed at the pleading in the man's eyes, the flat message written all over his face.

"Christ," he said, "I'm outnumbered. You're all spoiled rotten."

"You'll take us, then?" ventured Linda, pressing the advantage she felt in Bolt's off-handed admission of surrender.

"Jared," said Tom, "we could just ride on over there in the buggy or by ourselves."

"That cinches it then," said Bolt, "but I want you to know that we're being set up. I'll bet you dollars to bear claws that Jessie Belle has the prettiest women this side of the Pecos and probably a fancy whorehouse that makes us look like

22

poor nephews at a will-reading. We'll go, but don't blame me if you come back with long faces. That woman is out for hide, and she don't care how she scrapes it off."

Tom let out a shout, but he was drowned out by the chorus of shrieks from the six harlots who had shared supper with them. Penrod pounded on Bolt's back, knocking the breath from Jared's lungs. Hacking and coughing, Bolt slid away from the back-pounding, got to his feet.

"Get the horses hitched up to the buggy, Tom, and I'll saddle up my horse."

"Oh, good," cried Linda. "We'll change clothes real fast."

"No need to," Bolt said. "You girls look beautiful just the way you are."

"Don't be silly, Bolt," Abby giggled as she got up from the table. "We wouldn't think of going to a party in these plain old house dresses."

"Boy oh boy," grinned Tom as the girls dashed out of the room. "I can't wait to see the look on Jessie Belle's face when we show up."

"I'm sure it will be one of extreme satisfaction," said Bolt wryly. "It'll be a gloat, unless I miss my guess."

Tree frogs croaked, mosquitoes sang as the surrey rattled over the road toward Jessie Belle's. Tom drove the team. Bolt rode a newly broke horse that needed some seasoning. The night was clear, starry, fragrant with the lush smell of prairie flowers. The girls were singing "Buffalo Gals" and laughing. Tom smacked at his face every so often, trying to splatter a mosquito that flew by his ear looking for blood.

The pale moonlight shimmered across the land and ringed the buggy in its glow. Wearing a clean white shirt, Bolt looked like a white knight as he rode tall in the saddle ahead of the bouncing surrey. The silhouette of his Stetson was the only thing that broke that image.

"Looks like the damned circus is in town," Bolt said a few minutes later, when he saw the glittering lights up ahead.

"What'd you say?" Tom shouted from his perch on the buggy seat.

Bolt slowed his horse down until Tom drove the buggy up beside him. Linda and Abby, the two girls who sat on the seat beside Tom, stopped singing and leaned forward.

"I said it looks like a damned circus up ahead," Bolt shouted above the spontaneous laughter that erupted inside the carriage as the other girls finished singing the last chorus of their song. "Look at all those damned lamps. Most of them red lanterns."

"It figures," Tom said. "And look at the size of that damned sign Jessie's put up on the road. No way a feller's gonna miss the entrance to The Proud Peacock. I told you so."

"You need a sign like that," Abby said, her eyes wide with excitement as she stared at the big slab of wood that bore the legend: THE PROUD PEACOCK. BEAUTIFUL, EXOTIC GIRLS WHO WILL SATISFY EVERY NEED OF

EVERY MAN WHO ENTERS.

"I don't need anything but you girls and a clean, honest bordello." Bolt smiled, even though the sight of the gawdy sign irritated him. He was beginning to develop a strong hatred for the woman who called herself Jessie Belle.

The other girls poked their heads out the window openings of the carriage and began chattering in excited voices.

"Abby could be right," Tom said. "We could use a new sign and a few red lanterns around it."

"Word of mouth is worth a dozen signs," Bolt said. He gave his friend a dirty look and took the lead again. He angled his horse onto the brightly lit path that led to the old Campbell place and was immediately aware of the sounds of music and gaiety that drifted his way from the new bordello. Hanging lanterns glowed brightly from newly-planted posts that were spaced ten feet apart along the short path. The buggy creaked behind him, but the sound was lost in the increasing din from the bordello as he got closer.

As he rounded the last bend in the path, Bolt was dazzled by the light from all the lanterns that lit the front of Lem's old house. The area around the house was almost as bright as broad daylight, and he squinted from the glare. He wasn't surprised to see the large number of horses lined up at the two crowded hitchrails. Twenty-five or thirty horses, at least. The twin hitchrails stood where there had only been a single tilting hitching post before.

The old ranch house didn't look at all familiar

to Bolt. Instead of being dilapidated and weatherbeaten as it had been when Campbell lived there, new planks of wood covered the whole front of the house. The old sagging porch had been torn down and in its place was a wide, sweeping porch where more than a dozen men milled around, drink glasses in hand. Jessie was serious about putting him out of business.

"Ohhhh, look what they've done with Lem's house," Abby Mason squealed when Tom stopped the buggy near the fence, away from the other horses. "It's all so new and pretty. Lem would be surprised."

"He sure would be," Bolt laughed.

While Tom hitched the horses and buggy to a fence post, Bolt helped the girls down from the carriage. He didn't much like it that they'd worn such low-cut, clinging party gowns for the opening of Jessie Belle's whorehouse, but he didn't voice his objections. He didn't put any rules or regulations on them.

"I hope the fellers don't mistake you girls for Miss Belle's whores," he said to Cathy Boring, whose red dress was particularly bold and provocative, the way it clung to her sensuous curves.

"Oh, this gown," Cathy laughed as she took Bolt's hand and stepped out of the buggy. "We thought we could drum up some business for the Rocking Bar Bordello by wearing these."

Linda Ramsey fluffed her blond curls and gave Bolt a suggestive smile. "Pretty sneaky of us to use the grand opening of The Proud Peacock to promote your place, isn't it?"

26

"Well, I'm glad to know you're all so loyal to me and Tom," Bolt smiled. "You may change your mind after you've seen Miss Belle's fancy whorehouse."

"Never," Linda teased with a dramatic flair. "You've done right by us and we've got no intention of going over to the other side."

"That's right," Cathy chimed in, "but I want to see what those other girls look like."

"Then let's get to it," Bolt said.

A fellow leaning on the porch railing watched them as they headed toward the house. The fellow, who was dressed like a cattle drover, turned and said something to the man next to him. The man turned around and a big, lustful smile played across his lips when he saw Bolt's girls. Before long, all of the men on the porch turned to stare as Bolt and Tom and their entourage of six sensually-clad harlots made their way up the newly built steps.

"Bring on the girls," shouted a rough-looking chap who elbowed his way to the porch railing to get a closer look at the girls.

"Salvation is ours," cried another fellow, an old duffer who raised both arms to the skies. "The gods have provided us with more whores."

Two of Bolt's girls giggled as they strolled across the porch behind Bolt and Tom. Cathy Boring batted her eyes and wiggled her hips as she passed by the hooting men. Dusky-skinned Doris Fletcher thrilled the gawkers with a sultry look.

"I'll take the blonde," said the crude fellow who

27

looked like a cattle drover.

"Sorry, gentlemen, we're not for hire tonight," cooed Linda Ramsey.

A chorus of protesting chants went up from the disappointed men.

"Not tonight," Linda said in a teasing voice. "But you can find us just the road at the Rocking Bar Bordello any other night of the week. Stop by there and we'll be happy to pleasure you."

"I'll be there tomorrow night," shouted the one who looked like a cattle drover. "Keep it hot for me, honey."

"You've got a lot of guts," Bolt whispered to Linda just before they stepped through the open door into the noisy bordello. Cigar smoke hung heavy in the crowded room and the strong stench of it mingled with the overpowering, heady fragrance of perfume, the odor of spilled beer.

"Well, it isn't fair of that bitch to try to put us out of business," Linda said, an angry look of determination in her usually soft blue eyes. "If she wants trouble, she's going to get it."

The fellow who dressed like a cattle drover came in the door and Bolt waited until the man had walked on by them before he answered Linda.

"Don't take it so personally," he laughed as he scanned the room looking for Jessie Belle. "You're here to have fun and observe, not to work." He didn't spot Miss Belle in the crowd, but saw two scantily-dressed girls, obviously Jessie's whores, and wondered how many girls she had working for her. He had to admit that the two whores were stunning beauties. Both were dark-haired, dark-eyed and looked like they might have Spanish blood in them. Mexicans, maybe. One girl was tall with long, graceful legs that were fully visible from where he stood. The other was not quite as tall and her legs were hidden from view by the cluster of men who were gathered around both girls.

Abby Mason sidled up to Bolt, touched his arm.

"Oh, Bolt, isn't it beautiful in here?" she sighed. "I can't believe this living room is so big now. Just look what they've done to fix up Lem's old drab house. Isn't it pretty?"

"Yeah, I reckon, if you like all that frill and glitter." But Bolt could see that the inside of the house was much the same as it had been when Lem Campbell lived there. They'd torn down the faded curtain that had separated the living room from Lem's big bedroom and had made it into one large room, but they hadn't bothered to chink up the gaps between the rotting boards of the inside walls.

He knew that Jessie Belle and her workers had added a false front to the house to give visitors a good first impression and then filled the inside of the house with garish decorations to hide the shabby interior. He saw that Lem's old raggedy window curtains had been replaced with heavy white curtains which were held in place with gold rope sashes. Jessie must have gotten a bargain on the gaudy gold rope when she bought it, he thought, because she had used it profusely throughout the room: as sashes at all of the

29

windows, as picture frames around cheap paintings of nude women, and as decoration on the mantel above the fireplace and around several baskets of fresh-cut flowers that adorned the room. Hell, she had even threaded it around the banister that led upstairs.

Bolt noticed other things, too. Lem's old braided rug had been replaced by fancy Oriental rugs that appeared more threadbare than the braided one. And they had saved Lem's old sofa and comfortable chairs, added another sofa to the sitting area. Even though brightly colored afghans covered the four pieces of furniture, Bolt could picture the frayed and badly stained upholstery that he knew was still beneath the crocheted coverlets.

His attention was diverted to the stairway where one of the dark-haired whores was leading the smirking cattle drover upstairs, presumably to the cribs where she would ply her trade.

Bolt smiled. He didn't want to spend much time at The Proud Peacock, but he hoped he was still there when the cattle drover came back down. Bolt's curiosity was aroused and he could tell a lot about a whore by the expression on her customer's face after she had pleasured him. And he would be willing to bet that despite the whore's dark, sultry look, she was as cold as ice.

He spotted Jessie Belle then, at the very same time she noticed him from across the crowded room. A brief, wide-eyed look of surprise, or panic, he couldn't tell which, crossed her face when she saw him, but she quickly regained her composure and smiled at him as she began to thread her way through the knotted clusters of men.

Bolt was startled, too, because Jessie looked so different from the high-spirited, plainly-dressed, gun-totin' woman who had ridden hell bent for leather toward them that afternoon, shooting wildly at him and Tom as she rode. Jessie wore a shimmering, blue satin gown, cinched so tight at the waistline that it seemed to squeeze her full breasts up over the top of the low-cut bodice. Her bright red hair hung in long tight curls, pulled back away from her pinched face and held in place with a big, blue satin bow at the back of her head. Except for the two or three layers of makeup she'd slapped on her face, she looked more like a sixteen-year-old debutante from San Francisco than a grown woman.

Bolt had taken only two steps into the room when a big brute of a man stepped out in front of him, blocking his way. The giant flexed his muscles, glared at Bolt as if he were a bug to be squashed, and made it quite obvious that Bolt and his group were not welcome at The Proud Peacock.

# CHAPTER THREE

The ape-like man was more than a foot taller than Bolt and had a barrel chest that stretched his tent-like shirt to the limit, nearly popping the buttons. His arms were as big as hog bellies, his hands like ham hocks.

"Pardon me, sir," Bolt said as he tried to go around the giant. His head tilted back as he looked up into the ugly, mean face of the man who towered over him. There wasn't a strand of hair on the brute's head, not as much as a whisker on his face. The grotesque purple scar across his wide cheek seemed to pulse with a heartbeat of its own. He had thick, snarling lips and teeth that looked like they could easily bite Bolt's head off.

Tom Penrod stepped up beside his friend as the six frightened harlots huddled in behind them.

"What the hell . . ." Tom Penrod said as he tried to push his way through.

"Where in the hell do you think you're going, sonny?" growled the big brute. With no effort at all, he pushed Tom backward with the massive palm of his hand.

Tom staggered back and came up fighting mad,

his fists clenched.

"Forget it, Tom," Bolt said. He grabbed Tom's hand before he could throw a punch.

"You'd better listen to your friend," the enormous man boomed in a deep voice. He glared down at Bolt with beady eyes. "You can't come in here with those shameless hussies. This is a private party and we got our own whores."

Bolt glanced to the side and saw Jessie Belle coming his way.

"Evidently your boss forgot to tell you that she extended us a personal invitation," he said.

"You and your hot-headed friend, maybe," the big bouncer said as he looked the girls up and down. "But not those wicked wenches you brought with you. Miss Belle sure as hell wouldn't invite them."

"Miss Belle invited all of us," Bolt said, his voice cold and even.

The giant crossed his arms across his massive chest and didn't budge. The butt of his big pistol, a Colt, stuck out from his waistline.

"It's all right, Brutus," said Jessie Belle as she waltzed up, her long red curls bouncing across her shoulders. "These people are my guests."

Bolt watched Jessie Belle as she spoke with authority to the big man. She wore too much jewelry for her small size, he thought. Besides the rows of gold and pearl necklaces around her neck and the clanking gold bracelets on both wrists, she wore long dangling, gold and pearl earrings that twirled when she moved her head and that looked heavy enough to stretch her ear lobes out of shape. She also wore two large, gaudy rings, one on each hand, that seemed to dwarf her slender fingers.

Bolt wondered if Jessie Belle was not a lot like Lem's old house. A false front to present a good first impression. Garish decorations to hide a shabby interior.

"All of 'em?" Brutus whined. "The brazen tarts, too?"

"Yes? I invited them," Jessie said. "I thought it would do them some good to see what real whores looked like."

"You're the boss, lady," Brutus grumbled.

"That's right, Brutus," she said. "I want to have a word with you. Wait for me over at the bar."

Brutus glared at Bolt and Tom, gave the girls a wilting look. He finally dropped his arms, shrugged his massive shoulders, then turned and shuffled away, a sour look on his face.

Jessie smiled at Bolt. "Brutus is a good man. He's just doing his job," she said. "Please make yourselves at home. I'll be right back."

Before she could turn away, a tall, handsome man approached them.

"You gentlemen will have to check your guns and your hats," the lanky, wiry, dark-haired man said. He held out his hands and waited.

"This is Lyly Watley, one of my men," Jessie explained.

"Our hats?" Bolt said. "I can understand the guns, but why the hats?"

"We've learned from experience that men are less likely to start a fight if they're not wearing hats," Jessie said. "Must be that a hat makes them feel real important, real tough and manly, but it worked in my other whorehouse, and it's the rule here."

"How come he's wearing a hat and a piece?" Tom said sarcastically. He nodded toward Watley.

"Because he's not going to start a fight. He works for me. Lyle, this is Jared Bolt and Tom Penrod. They own the Rocking Bar bordello up the road."

"I'll take your weapons and your Stetsons, gentlemen, and then you can come on in," Lyle said, his hands still outstretched.

"I thought we were your guests," Bolt said to Jessie.

"You are," she smiled arrogantly, "just like all of the other nice gentlemen in here who have already complied with my orders. And, quite frankly, of all the men at my party tonight, you two are the ones I'm most concerned about removing your weapons before you go any farther."

"A fine way to treat your guests," Tom grumbled. "Like goddamned outlaws."

"I'm sure you can understand," Jessie hissed. "After all, I did shoot at you today. You might be here to seek revenge."

"That's bullshit," Tom said.

"Nevertheless, we are now competitors, and I figure you're itching to destroy my business before I can do you much harm. Men have been known to kill over such things."

"Women, too, it appears," Bolt said dryly. "You don't have to take our guns, Miss Belle. We won't be staying."

"No need to get huffy. I want you to stay and see what class and elegance is all about."

"I've seen enough, ma'am."

Bolt saw Jessie bristle.

"It's Miss Belle to you. Don't ever call me ma'am again," she said through tight lips.

"Are you staying or leaving?" Lyle asked, his listless tone of voice reflecting his boredom. "Makes no difference to me, but if you're staying, I need your weapons."

Bolt took his hat off, brushed the dust off it, then slid it back into position, squared it up. "We ain't stayin'."

"It's all right, Lyle," Jessie said after a brief hesitation. "Let my guests keep their guns and hats. I'm sure they won't cause any trouble tonight. I'm sure Mister Bolt is smart enough to know that he would ruin his reputation if he tried anything in front of all these people. I'll take my chances."

Bolt detested the bitch for saying such a thing, but he was fascinated by her manipulations, her vacillation back and forth between phony pleasantness and downright rudeness. When he saw Lyle Watley turn and walk away without another word, it was a further indication that Jessie was in total control of everything and everyone connected with The Proud Peacock.

"I must talk to Brutus for a minute," she said. "I'll be back in a minute to show you around. In the meantime, please come in and have some champagne. It might improve your disposition."

36

Bolt watched her swish across the floor as she headed for the long bar that had been built at one end of Lem's old living room. Brutus had his back to her and when she walked up behind him, she reached up and grabbed him by one of his massive arms and Bolt thought he could see her dig her fingers into the brute's flesh. When Brutus turned to face her, she spoke to him harshly, a stern scowl on her face. Although Bolt couldn't hear her words above the din of the crowded room, he knew Jessie was giving Brutus a tongue lashing about something.

"She's giving him hell," he laughed.

"Yeah," said Tom. "I'd hate to run into either one of those two on a dark, lonely road."

"I know what you mean."

"In fact, I don't know which one of them would frighten me more."

"I think you'd be least stand a fighting chance with the brute," Bolt said wryly.

"So do I," Tom chuckled. "That little woman has already shown us that she'd shoot a man down without batting an eyelash."

The muffled scream came from upstairs.

Bolt saw Jessie glance toward the stairway briefly, but she continued talking to Brutus. It was so noisy downstairs that nobody else in the room seemed to notice the eerie wail.

But Bolt heard it and felt a chill creep across his flesh.

Linda Ramsey heard it, too.

"What was that?" she asked as she snuggled close to Bolt. "A woman's scream?"

"No," Bolt said. "It was a man's scream."

Linda's face went white.

Bolt looked at Jessie again and saw that she was still talking to Brutus. He wondered why she didn't go to investigate.

The flesh of Brutus' thick neck stretched taut as he nodded to Jessie Belle after her brief talk with him. He ran a massive hand across his bald head, then turned and headed for the stairway, apparently with a new purpose in mind, or another chore to do for his boss lady. Perhaps Jessie was sending him to check on things upstairs.

A minute later, Jessie swished across the floor toward Bolt and his friends,, her blue satin gown shimmering in the flickering light of the lanterns suspended from the rafters. The heavy scent of her perfume reached Bolt before she did.

"I'm sorry about the misunderstanding," she said. "I hope Brutus didn't frighten you."

"Not at all," Bolt said as he watched Brutus lumber up the steps. "He's a mighty big man, though, and I can see where he might be intimidating to some folks."

Jessie smiled, but Bolt noticed the way she clenched her hands together. Did she have something to be nervous about, he wondered. Had she heard the scream, too? He was sure she had. Was something funny going on in her whorehouse that she didn't want him to know about? Did she and her whores cater to men who got some strange sexual satisfaction from pain? Whatever it was that caused her to be fidgety, it was obvious to Bolt that Jessie Belle was suddenly uncomfortable with his presence in her bordello.

"I should have told Brutus you were coming," she said with a haughty flip of her head, "but, quite frankly, I didn't think you'd show up. I mean, the way you talked this afternoon . . ."

"No need to apologize. We changed our minds."

"I'm glad you did." She took a long hard look at the six harlots who stood behind Bolt and Tom. "I must admit that your whores are fairly attractive. Turn around and let me have a look at you, girl," she said to dusky-skinned Doris Fletcher.

Doris hesitated for only a moment before she did as she was told, a puzzled look on her face. She whirled around slowly until she faced Miss Belle again.

"Not bad," Jessie said. She then motioned Linda Ramsey to twirl around for inspection. "You next, blondie." When Linda didn't respond to her demands, Jessie didn't push it. "Yes, your whores are rather pretty, Bolt, but of course they don't measure up to my girls in poise and beauty, culture, elegance, sensuality and in so many other important ways."

"I reckon we all got our own opinions about such things." Bolt rankled at Jessie's attitude toward his girls, at her crudeness in treating them like so much horse flesh on auction day, but he didn't kick up a fuss. His harlots were independent enough to stand on their own two feet, as Linda had done. Not only that, he wanted to see what Jessie was up to.

"Please, come and have some champagne," Jessie said graciously. "All of you."

"No thanks," Bolt said. "We're not staying that long."

"But you just got here. You should stay long enough to meet all of my girls. I think you'll see what I mean about them."

"I'll take your word for it, Miss Belle. We just came by to be neighborly and to wish you luck with your new business."

"You don't really mean that, Mister Bolt."

"Yes, I do. There are plenty of randy men around to support two bordellos."

"Aw, Bolt, I thought we were going to stay here for a little while," Tom said, a dejected look on his face. "I'd kinda like to see what Miss Belle's other girls look like."

"You can stick around if you want to, Tom. I just don't like crowds."

"I'd like your whores to stay," Jessie said. "They're pretty enough to add some atmosphere of sexuality to The Proud Peacock while my girls are busy. And they can keep my customers entertained while the lecherous bastards are waiting their turns. If any of your girls play the piano, that would help keep the party lively so the fellows don't get bored."

"Yeah, the fellows will get restless after a while," Bolt said with a knowing nod of his head. "I can see where my girls could liven things up for you, keep the customers' blood running hot. That's what you mean, isn't it?"

"Yes," said Jessie. "Your whores wouldn't have to do anything more than what dance hall gals do. You know, they could just talk to the men real sweet, maybe be a little seductive to keep them aroused."

"And do you plan to pay my girls for their services?" Bolt stroked his chin and gave Jessie a long hard look.

"What services?" Jessie demanded, obviously outraged at Bolt's suggestion. "You expect me to pay your whores just for sitting around and talking to the men?"

"That's what I had in mind."

"Absolutely not," Jessie raged. "After all, I'm not asking them to sleep with the customers. That's what my girls are getting paid for."

"That's what I thought," Bolt said. "On behalf of my girls, I'll have to decline your offer."

"Your gals just might enjoy it. Did you think of that? This is a grand opening party, after all, and I'd think your whores would welcome the opportunity to attend a party as guests instead of as slaves, like they usually are."

Bolt stiffened. "My girls aren't slaves."

Jessie laughed nervously. "You know what I mean."

"No, I don't know what you mean." Bolt looked Jessie directly in the eyes.

"You're being contrary, Mister Bolt. I think you're purposely trying to irritate me."

"Nope."

"I thought you wanted to be neighborly."

Bolt heard her voice soften, and knew she was trying to use her womanly ways to get her way.

"I do, but that doesn't include letting my girls work for you with no pay."

41

"I knew it," Jessie snapped. "Your whores are cowering slaves, after all. Just look at them. It's obvious that you control their every move. You won't even let them enjoy my gala party."

Bolt liked to see the sparks of fire in Jessie's eyes when she got riled up. He knew she struggled to be pleasant to him, but she couldn't help herself from reverting to her natural state of rudeness. He wondered how much taunting it would take to make her explode.

"I'm not controlling them," he said. "I'm just protecting them."

"Ha! They're mindless sluts who are afraid to voice their own opinions. You won't even let them have a little fun while they're here." As she ranted on, Jessie's face flushed crimson.

"It's up to them. My harlots are free to do whatever they want to." Bolt glanced back. "What do you say, girls? Do you want to stay here for a little while and mingle with the guests?"

"No," said Linda Ramsey. "I'm quite uncomfortable here." The other girls shook their heads in response to Bolt's question.

"It's unanimous, Miss Belle," Bolt said. "The girls don't want to stay."

Tom stepped forward. "How many whores you got here, Jezebel?" he asked.

"It's Jessie Belle," she said coldly. "I've got three girls right now."

"Only three?"

"Yes. Maria, over there," she said as she pointed to the Spanish-looking harlot, "the one who's going upstairs with that cowboy. The other two girls are busy with customers. Are you interested?"

"Not interested enough to wait in line."

"They're worth waiting for."

"No thanks."

"I'll have more girls working here before the end of the week."

"Good." Tom yawned as if bored to tears. "Well, goodbye and good luck, Miss Jezebel. It's almost my bedtime."

"So early?" Jessie sneered. "A young, virile lad like you?"

"Yep," Tom laughed. "Even a randy bastard like me has got to get some sleep. We all get up with the chickens over at the Rocking Bar Ranch. There's a lot of work to raisin' cattle and we got to get an early start every mornin'."

"That's right," said Bolt. "Thank you for inviting us."

"I really wish you'd stay," Jessie said, turning pleasant again.

Bolt knew that Jessie wasn't sincere. She was nervous as hell and she wanted all of them out of there as quickly as possible. He had wanted to stick around long enough to see the cattle drover's face when he came downstairs after being with Jessie's whore, but he really didn't care about it any more. He wondered, though, if the drover had been the one who'd screamed. The eerie cry still haunted him, still nagged at his mind. The scream he'd heard was definitely a man's wail, and it was a wail of agony, not ecstasy.

43

"You'd better get back to your paying customers, Miss Belle," he said. "You ain't gonna make any money off us."

"Just call me Jessie." She smiled and offered her hand. "Goodbye. Thank you for coming."

Bolt shook the small, slender hand briefly, then let it drop.

"By the way, Jessie, I head someone scream a few minutes ago. Did you hear it?"

"Why, no, I didn't."

Her eyes widened as if she were surprised, but Bolt knew better. He knew she'd heard the scream as well as he had. In fact, it was just after he'd heard the muffled scream that Jessie had become nervous and fidgety.

"Do your customers manhandle the whores much? Slap them around?" He watched her carefully and she seemed relieved at his question.

"Some. Men get drunk, they get mean. It goes with the territory. You ought to know that."

"Not at the Rocking Bar Bordello. I don't allow anybody to rough up my girls."

"Oh mercy me. Aren't we pious?"

"Not pious. I just believe in protecting my girls. I don't think they'd cotton to the type of customer you seem to attract."

"Don't concern yourself with it, Mister Bolt. It was a man who screamed, not one of my whores."

"Oh? How do you know? I thought you didn't hear the scream." Bolt's eyes narrowed with an accusing stare and he felt a certain sense of satisfaction as he watched Jessie squirm.

She stammered something then blurted out, "I

44

didn't hear anybody scream, dammit. You're trying to put words in my mouth. Personally, I think you're imagining things, but if anyone screamed, it damned sure wasn't one of my whores. It had to be one of the men crying out to the throes of his climax. Men are such damned fools when it comes to sex. They let their peckers do their thinking. But I'm not complaining. That's why we're both in the business, to make money off the lust-crazed men."

"That's one woman's opinion. Goodbye, Miss Belle." Thoroughly disgusted by her attitude, Bolt started to turn away.

"Remember, Mister Bolt, I'm going to put you out of business," Jessie snarled, her eyes full of hatred and bitterness.

"Better people than you have tried, Miss Belle," he said as he looked her directly in the eye.

"Maybe so, but none as ruthless as I am."

"I believe that, ma'am," he said as he turned on his heels.

"And don't ma'am me," she shouted.

Bolt ducked instinctively as he walked out the door, half-way expecting her to throw something at him.

"What a spitfire she is," Tom said as he and the girls followed Bolt out the door.

"She's lying," Bolt said to Tom as they walked to the horses and buggy. "The bitch is damned sure lying. Linda heard the scream and you heard the man scream, didn't you?"

"Yeah, I heard it, but what the hell? It ain't none of our concern."

45

"I know. I should let it go and forget about the damned bitch."

"You should, but you won't," Tom grumbled. "I know you too well. Your damned curiosity is gonna get you in deep shit this time. I can already smell it."

# CHAPTER FOUR

Bolt didn't realize how tense he'd been until he reined Nick onto the Rocking Bar Ranch property and saw the glow of lamplight at the windows of his ranch house. It was then that he felt his shoulder muscles relax, as if a great weight had suddenly been lifted off them.

The house would be neat and tidy, he knew, the dishes washed and put away. Harmony Sanchez had been wise to stay at home and putter around the house. Being a whorehouse madam herself, and a strong-willed one at that, she probably would have tangled with Jessie Belle tooth and nail. Literally.

Harmony Sanchez considered Bolt's harlots her own responsibility and because she thought of them as family, it gave her a great deal of satisfaction to take care of them and protect them from the evils of their occupation. She mothered those gals like a clucking hen, even though, at twenty-four, she was only a couple of years older than they were. She'd be the first one to kick a fellow in the balls if he harmed as much as a hair on the head of any one of the girls.

Although Harmony usually slept with the girls

in the bordello, which was down the hill from the ranch house, she also shared Bolt's bed at those times when it was right for both of them. Usually on Sunday nights, when she didn't have to work.

It was Sunday night, Bolt thought, but it was almost too much to hope that she would be there to sleep with him tonight when he wanted her so much. He imagined that she would already be asleep in her bedroom in the bordello, figuring that he and the others would be out late.

He rode on by the house and down the hill to the stable. He glanced over at the bordello and was filled with a sudden sense of disappointment, a quiet desperation, when he saw the lamplight filtering through the gingham curtains at the windows. Harmony would be there. He could stop by the big rustic cabin that served as the bordello and invite her to go back up to the house with him, but he wouldn't do that. If she wanted him, she'd wait for him, no matter how late the hour.

He dismounted near the stable, glanced back and saw the carriage coming down the gentle slope. By the time the buggy clanked to a stop, rocking on its hinges, he had lit the hurricane lamp that hung outside the stable and another one inside.

While Tom was busy unhitching the wagon, Bolt helped the girls down.

"Well, are you glad you went over to The Proud Peacock?" he asked.

"In a way, yes," said Linda Ramsey. "At least we got to see what our competition is like. And from what I saw, I don't think we have a damned thing to worry about."

"I don't either," said Tom. He slapped his hands against his trousers to brush the dust off them. "I sure as hell wasn't impressed by The Proud Peacock and I like Jezebel even less than I did before."

"She's a haughty old witch," Doris Fletcher said as she took Bolt's hand and stepped down.

"If you felt that way about her, how come you let her boss you around? Why did you turn around like a damned puppet for her?"

"I . . . I don't know. Because she told me to, I guess."

"And do you always do what other people tell you to do, dammit?"

"Well, no," she said timidly, almost in tears. "You're mad at me, aren't you, Bolt?"

"Not mad, Doris, just disappointed that you would allow that little bitch to order you around like that. I know you had to keep your mouth shut and do whatever you were told when you worked in Denver, but you work for me now, and you don't have to do anything you don't want to. Ever."

"I know," she said. "I just can't get used to being treated like a real woman. When you become a whore, you expect to be treated like a whore. You lose all self-respect. You just don't understand what it's like."

"No, but I do know that you gals are a lot more decent than some of the snobbish society women I know." He put his arm around her, gave her a quick squeeze. "You've got all the freedom you want here, Doris, and I hope you'll learn to use it."

"I will," she smiled.

"Good," Bolt said. "And that goes for all of you girls. Use your freedom, or lose it. And with that bit of fatherly advice, I'll say goodnight."

"Goodnight, Bolt," the girls said in unison.

"I'll walk them over to the bordello," Tom said. "Say goodnight to Harmony if she's still up."

As Bolt strolled up the moonlit path to the ranch house, a terrible feeling of loneliness tugged at his heart. He wanted so much to be with Harmony tonight and forget all about Jessie Belle and her damned whorehouse. But he couldn't get that cold-hearted bitch out of his mind, even though his stomach churned with disgust whenever he thought about how she treated other people — men and women alike.

He had wanted to interfere when she'd ordered Doris around, but he'd wanted to set an example for Jessie, let her know how he treated his girls. And more important than that, he didn't interfere because he knew Doris had to learn to stand up for herself. Doris was shy, intimidated, and more easily swayed than the other girls who worked for him, but in time, she would be as strong as they were and she would be able to say no to pushy people like Jessie Belle.

Jessie was a damned liar, he thought, a phony, a crude, cunning wench who had absolutely no respect for men. And yet, because of her greed, she took advantage of their lustful nature.

Maybe he took advantage of man's lustful nature, too, he thought, but he did it because he felt there was a need for prostitutes. They serves the lonely men, the unhappy, married men, and fellows who might otherwise vent their sexual frustrations by raping young, innocent girls if they didn't have prostitues. Maybe his reasons for running a bordello were no better than Jessie's. He didnt' know.

He stopped on the path long enough to listen to the croaking frogs and put Jessie Belle out of his mind. He drank in a deep breath of the cool night air and reminded himself how lucky he was to live out in the open spaces where neighbors were far enough away that they could be ignored, which was exactly what he planned to do about Jessie.

He paused again at the bottom of the porch and looked up at the stars. A cloud skittered across the face of the moon and blotted out its light for a brief moment. He wished for rain. They needed it for the garden. But one little cloud would not bring a drop of moisture to the fields. He took another deep breath and hoped he would feel more optimistic in the morning.

His boots clacked against the planks as he walked up the steps. He stopped at the back door long enough to wipe his boots on the small braided rug outside so he wouldn't track dirt in the house.

The door swung open when he was looking down at the rug, and he nearly jumped out of his skin.

"Oh, Harmony. Jeez, you startled me."

Harmony laughed and to sounded like a dozen

musical bells ringing.

"Do I look that bad?" She fluffed her golden blond hair and gave him a teasing look.

"No, you look damned good to me, you little hussy." He stepped inside, kicked the door shut, and took her in his arms, kissed her hard. He stepped back and looked at her. "Oh, boy, you look good to me. You make a tired man's blood boil hot."

"Maybe you should go to The Proud Peacock more often," she laughed.

"Never again." He saw that she was wearing her pale blue robe, the one he liked because it had no buttons, but only a sash to hold it in place as it wrapped around her soft curves.

The robe was soft to his touch as he took her in his arms again and hugged her tight. He nuzzled his face into the smooth curve of her neck, kissed her there. She smelled of crushed, dried flowers on an autumn afternoon, and her delicate, heady scent made his knees go weak.

"I'm so glad you're here, Harmony," he said as he peppered her neck with kisses.

"Are you?" Her voice had a soft husk to it.

"Yes, you smell so good."

"And you smell like a whorehouse." She stepped back and crinkled her nose.

"That bad, huh?"

"That bad." She reached down and slid her hand in his and they walked together into the kitchen. "You want a drink?"

"Yes. A little brandy to wash the bad taste out of my mouth." He opened the cupboard and brought out a bottle of good brandy. "You want some?"

"No thank you," she said as she put a tumbler down on the counter in front of him. "You look worried, Bolt."

He poured just a little brandy in the glass and drank it down in one swallow. He sighed and felt a warm glow in his stomach, partly from the brandy and partly because of the way he felt about Harmony.

"Not worried. Just disgusted that someone like that ruthless bitch, Jessie Belle, thinks she can put me out of business."

Harmony gave him a reassuring pat on the shoulder.

"She won't last very long if she's as bad as you say she is."

"She's worse. I don't even want to think about her. What I really need is a bath. I feel dirty after being over there at her gaudy pig sty."

When he entered his tidy bedroom a few minutes later, he saw that Harmony had already turned the bed down. She was some woman. Always there when he needed her, and yet she never demanded his attention when he needed to be alone. And she seemed to sense that delicate difference in his moods. She never harped at him or questioned him, although he was sure she knew about the other women who drifted in and out of his life.

As he stepped out of his clothes, he thought how lucky he was to have a strong, sensitive woman like Harmony at his side. He watched her as she stood at the dressing table, her back to him, and felt his heart swell with the strong, deep feelings of love he had for her at such times.

Naked, he walked over and slipped his arms around her shoulders, slid his hands down the outside of her robe and felt the mounds of her swollen breasts beneath the soft fabric. He looked at her reflection in the mirror and smiled.

She unfastened the sash around her waist and let her robe fall open.

"Did I ever tell you how beautiful you are?" he husked as he kissed the back of her smooth neck. Her fragile, flowery scent drifted up to his nostrils and caused chill bumps to rise on his flesh. He shivered and then felt a warm glow flood through his loins. His cock began to swell.

"Yes, but you can say it again." She turned around to face him and tucked into the folds of his arms, pressed her body against his.

"You're beautiful, Harmony. And you're the sweetest woman I've ever known."

He slid the robe off her shoulders, and reached for her full breasts. She dropped her arms, let the robe fall to the floor.

"Oh, Bolt, I love you so much," she whispered as she pressed her body against his.

Their bare flesh came together and when his swollen member touched the furry mound of her sex, the damp, silken flesh of her slit, he shuddered again.

He held her tight and lowered his mouth to her sensually parted lips. They were soft and supple and he slid his tongue inside where it was warm and wet. She responded to his kiss by flicking her own tongue across his. He kissed her long and deeply, wanting her so bad, he ached from it.

"You're a very special woman," he said when their lips parted for a brief instant.

"And you're the best man I've ever known," she mumbled as his lips covered hers again.

Their embrace was complete, from their hot, supple lips, down to the flesh where her full breasts crushed against his chest, right on down to their gyrating hips, and their loins, where his throbbing cock probed at the slippery portal of her sex.

He gasped with the prickly sensation that flooded through his body and set every nerve ending on edge.

"I want you, Bolt," she said, a velvet husk to her soft voice. She spread her legs slightly, thrust up against him, urging him to enter her.

"Can you wait until we get to the bed?" he said, with a husk that matched her with its urgency.

She tugged at his arm and led him to the bed.

"Hurry," she said.

"You're a brazen hussy," he teased as they climbed in bed together.

"Yes, a hot, eager, shameless, brazen hussy," she said.

"I'm so glad you waited up for me tonight. I can't tell you how lonesome I felt when I saw the light in the bordello and thought you were down there, already asleep."

"I would have waited for you tonight, no matter how late it was when you got home." She ran her hand across his stomach and down to his crotch, where she took his thick cock in her hand and squeezed it.

"I knew you would."

She climbed over him and straddled his legs. Her breasts were within inches of his face and he reached up and took one in each hand. She stayed there, poised above him and he felt the heat of her sex flare out across his groin.

"I want you, Bolt," she said for the second time.

He looked up into her radiant face as she gazed down at him, her eyes glazed with desire. Again, he was overwhelmed by his growing love for her.

"I want you, too, Harmony. More than anyone I've ever known."

"I'm glad because you make me so happy."

He smiled and thought how vulnerable he was just then.

"If I'm not damned careful," he said, "I'm going to end up on my knees tonight."

"What?" she said as a puzzled look covered her face.

"Proposing marriage to you," he said.

"I'd say yes," she cooed.

"Then I'll be extra careful," he laughed.

"And I'll be extra sexy," she said as she lowered herself over his shaft.

# CHAPTER FIVE

Bolt saw the fancy carriage just as he was getting ready to turn the loaded buckboard off the main road and onto his own property. The carriage was coming toward him and he knew he'd have to stop before he made the turn. There wasn't enough room on the narrow path for the wagons to pass each other.

He reined back hard and his horse dug its hooves into the hard ground, spewing clouds of dust into the air. Bolt coughed and choked from the grit that got into his mouth and eyes. He blinked the grit away as the buckboard came to an abrupt stop. The wagon rocked back and forth, squeaking on its rusty hinges before it settled down.

Bolt didn't recognize the carriage and he wasn't close enough to make out the features of the man who was up in the driver's seat.

He'd been in San Antonio all day, picking up needed supplies and he was in no mood to talk to strangers. He had awakened early that morning with a renewed feeling of joy after spending the night with Harmony and forgetting all about Jessie Belle.

But as soon as he rode past the old Lem Campbell place on his way to town and saw that hideous sign out front with the unlit lanterns around it, his blood had begun to boil. The memories of Jessie Belle and The Proud Peacock had come flooding back in on him and from then on, that was all he could think about. At one point, he'd become so angry about her haughty attitude that he'd vowed to cut a new path to town just so he wouldn't have to ride past there again.

Tom had ridden to town later on his own horse and after they'd loaded the supplies on the buckboard, they ate lunch together at a small cafe. Bolt had headed back to the ranch, leaving Tom to do whatever he did in town.

The carriage eased out onto the road. Even at close range, as the carriage pulled up alongside him, heading toward town, Bolt didn't recognize the driver. He tipped his hat anyway and the driver returned the gesture.

"Good afternoon, Mister Bolt."

The voice came from inside the carriage and Bolt knew who it was, even before he glanced back. His temper flared and rose to the point of explosion. The nerve of that damned bitch.

She stuck her head out the carriage window and Bolt was momentarily blinded by the glint of the sun reflecting off her gold necklace. She wore a bright red dress that clashed with the carrot red of her hair and a floppy bonnet that looked too big for her small head.

"What in the hell are you doing over here, Miss Belle?" he said. "You're out of your territory, aren't you?"

"I came to call," she said, her voice sickeningly sweet.

"Fortunately for me, I wasn't home."

"And fortunately for me, I didn't come to call on you."

"Who then? What in the hell are you up to now?"

"You're quite rude, Mister Bolt. That's no way to talk to a lady."

"And you're no lady."

"That's one man's opinion," she said, tossing his own words back in his face.

Knowing that she was getting the upper hand, topping his sarcasm with her own barbs, Bolt relaxed his shoulder muscles and regained his composure.

"I hope you enjoyed your visit here, Miss Belle," he said, his tone of voice, if not friendly, at least polite.

"Oh, I certainly did, Mister Bolt. My visit was quite productive."

"What's that supposed to mean?" Bolt said, his irritation creeping up again.

"It means that I accomplished what I came to do."

Bolt didn't like the way she struck her nose up in the air. If it had been raining, she would have drowned.

"You can't talk with a straight tongue, can you?" he said.

"Your whores seem to think so."

Bolt's eyes narrowed to slits as he eyed her

suspiciously. "What are you doing talking to them?"

"Are they not allowed to talk to me?" she said smugly.

"Hell, yes, they can talk to any damned body they want to. I just want to know why you were talking to them."

"I told you, I came to call. Anything wrong with being neighborly?"

"Not a damned thing, but you ain't the type to be neighborly. You said so yourself."

"Maybe I had a change of heart," she said.

"You ain't got no heart to change."

"You're getting rude again, Mister Bolt."

Frustration raged through Bolt.

"What in the hell are you doing here, Miss Belle?" he demanded.

"You already asked that question."

"And I didn't get a straight answer. You're talking in circles. I know damned well you're up to no good. What are you trying to hide?"

"Nothing," Jessie said with that smug look. "You said your girls weren't slaves, and I assumed you allowed them their privacy. But if you insist on knowing what we talked about, I'll tell you. You'll know soon enough anyway."

"I wish you would."

"I offered them jobs at The Proud Peacock and two of your whores accepted."

Bolt felt like he'd been hit in the stomach with a sledge hammer.

"I don't believe you."

"First you tell me that I talk in circles and then

when I tell you the facts in simple words that even you should be able to understand, you call me a liar. I don't understand you."

"You had no right to come over here and try to steal my girls away from me."

"I'm not stealing them, Mister Bolt. They want to come over to The Proud Peacock."

"Bullshit."

"It seems you're the one who talks in circles. You say that your whores are free to make their own decisions and yet when they do, you raise a stink about it."

"What do you expect me to do about it, sit on my ass and say nothing?" Bolt roared. "You're a sneaky, ruthless bitch."

"I tried to warn you."

"You didn't have to. I knew it the first time I laid eyes on you."

"You're nothing but a blowhard, Mister Bolt, always patting yourself on the back, telling everyone how wonderful you are. You brag about how well you treat your harlots, but I can already tell by your rage, which is quite unbecoming, I must say, that you're going to try and stop your girls from coming to work for me. It's quite apparent that your whores have no freedom at all."

"They can go any damned place they want to. I just find it hard to believe that they would want to go over to your gaudy shack."

"Go ask them and see for yourself."

"Why in the hell would you want to come over here and take my girls?" Bolt asked.

"I need more whores and this is the easiest place to find them."

"That's a rotten reason."

"Maybe so," Jessie sneered, "but I've only got two whores left now."

"Oh?"

"One of my whores ran off this morning."

"How come?"

"Hell, how should I know?" Jessie cursed. "I knew the little tramp wouldn't last long. She complained that the work was too hard for her."

"Whoring is hard work," Bolt said, "especially with the kind of men you cater to. It takes a special woman to know how to pleasure a man in bed."

Jessie laughed haughtily. "You live in a dream world if you believe that romantic hogwash. It doesn't take anything special to be a whore. Hell, all she has to do is lie on her back, spread her legs and think of something else. The man does all the work. And if he doesn't go away satisfied, then it's his own damned fault."

Bolt cringed at Jessie Belle's words. He couldn't see how one woman could be so heartless. Even her pale hazel eyes seemed void of any feeling or emotion.

"Were you a whore once?" he said bluntly.

She stiffened and leaned back into the carriage, then popped her head back out. "Why would you ask such a rude question?"

"Just curious," he said. "Most madams were soiled doves in their earlier days."

Jessie's eyes flashed with anger. She glared at

him and looked like a fishwife.

"Are you insinuating that I'm too old and haggard to be a whore?" she snapped, her jaw muscles taut.

"I ain't insinuating anything, ma'am."

"That's what you're thinking, though, isn't it?" she said.

"Actually, I was thinking that you look pretty good for your age," Bolt grinned.

"What's that supposed to mean?" she demanded. "Never mind. I don't want to know. You're the meanest man I've known."

"Who, me?" Bolt's face had a look of pure innocence about it.

"You're just trying to make me mad."

"Evidently I don't have to try very hard. You got something stuck in your craw, lady, and I can't do anything abut it."

Jessie's face flushed bright red.

"As a matter of fact, I was a whore," she blurted. "And a damned good one. I was very good in bed."

"I wouldn't know anything about that."

"No, you wouldn't. And you never will. I wouldn't sleep with you if you got down on your knees and begged."

"I ain't beggin', ma'am."

"Oh, damned you, Bolt!"

"Which girls are you stealing from me?" he asked as the reality of what was happening set in. Doris Fletcher would be one of them, he was sure. She was still too easily influenced by others to resist someone as clever as Jessie.

"Doris Fletcher and Abby Mason, and with a little training, I think they'll make good whores."

He wasn't too surprised by the names she mentioned. Doris Fletcher was still too easily influenced by others, and Abby Mason had developed some sort of an attachment to Lem's old house, it seemed.

"They're good whores now," Bolt said coldly. "You'll ruin them."

"You're entitled to your own opinion, Mister Bolt, but I think they'll be almost as good as my whores within a week."

"They won't last that long at your place. I give them one night, if that."

"As I said, you're entitled to your own opinion. My driver will bring the carriage over in the morning to fetch them."

Bolt had forgotten all about the driver. He glanced back and saw the man sitting stiff in the seat, eyes straight ahead, the reins slack in his hand. He was just like the other dummies who worked for Jessie, Bolt thought. He did exactly what he was told and asked no questions.

"He may return with an empty carriage," he said.

"I don't think so. I've offered your whores a great deal more money than you pay them and I don't think they'll be changing their minds." She stuck her head farther out the window. "I'm ready to go now, James," she hollered.

The driver cracked the whip across the back of one of the horses and the buggy began to roll away.

Jessie waved at Bolt with a white-gloved hand and he was sickened by the smug smile on her face.

After they were gone, he pulled the buckboard onto his own path and went down the slope to the stable. He hopped down from the hard wooden seat and without stopping to put the supplies away, he dashed across the yard to the bordello.

Harmony opened the door for him.

"What's this nonsense about Doris and Abby working at The Proud Peacock?" he said as he went outside. He glanced around the room and saw only the four harlots who had not agreed to work for Jessie.

"You already know," Harmony said.

"Yes. I met up with Jessie at the road, but I can't believe Doris and Abby would go over and work for her."

"I know. I tried to convince the girls that they were making a mistake, but I guess Miss Belle's offer was too tempting."

"Isn't it terrible?" Linda Ramsey said as she and the other girls walked over. "We all tried to tell them they were doing wrong, but they wouldn't listen."

"How much did she offer them?" Bolt asked.

"Twice as much as you're paying them, a bonus of two dollars if they work Sundays, and another two-dollar bonus if they work seven days straight."

"She offered all of us the same," Linda said. "Miss Belle convinced Abby and Doris that if they worked every day, they'd make enough in a year to retire. She said that they'd still be young enough then to latch on to a husband."

"Jeez," said Bolt. "If they work every day, they'll be dead in a year, or so worn out no man would want them."

"That's not the worst part," Harmony said. "Jessie said the The Proud Peacock will be open twenty-four hours a day and that each girl will be expected to be available at least eighteen hours each day."

"Yeah," said Cathy Boring. "Miss Belle told them that they'd still have eight hours to sleep, but that doesn't leave any time for pleasure."

"It's slavery, Bolt," said Harmony. "Jessie kept telling them about all the money they would make, and she convinced them that there wouldn't be many customers during the day or late at night, so they actually wouldn't have to work that much. The only problem with that is that they get paid the same amount of money a day, whether they work only five or six hours during slow times, or the full eighteen hours."

"That bitch," Bolt snapped.

"She may be a bitch, but she's also very cunning. She can be very charming when she wants to be, and very persuasive. Doris and Abby are just too naive to see through her scam."

"Where are the girls now?"

"Upstairs. Packing their bags."

"I'm going to go up and have a talk with them," Bolt said.

"It won't do any good," said Cathy. "We've already told them all the reasons why they shouldn't go to work at The Proud Peacock."

"It won't do any harm."

"We can't force them to stay here if they don't want to," Harmony said.

"I know. You did what you could and I appreciate it."

Bolt took the steps two at a time. Both girls were in the same room, their open bags on the beds. Doris had a sheepish look on her face when she looked up and saw Bolt standing in the open doorway.

"You know you're both making a big mistake, don't you?" Bolt said.

"I'm sorry you're unhappy about this, Bolt," said Doris, "but we've made our decision and we're not going to change our minds."

"You don't know how bad it is over at Jessie's place," Bolt said.

"We've already heard all the reasons why we shouldn't go," said Abby. "I really like you and I'm sorry we've let you down."

"I don't care about that," Bolt said gently. "I care about both of you girls. I care about your safety, and your health."

"We'll be all right, Bolt," said Doris. "Jessie promised that Brutus would protect us."

"There's something that's not quite right over there," Bolt said.

"What's that?" Doris asked.

"I don't know," said Bolt. "I can't put my finger on it yet, but there's going to be big trouble over there. There's something evil about that place. I can feel it in my bones."

"Oh, that's sour grapes," said Abby. "You just want Jessie to have trouble. She's really very nice once you get to know her."

"The hell she is. She's a vicious woman and she'll turn you into slaves, like she has those other girls. She doesn't give a damn about you."

"Jessie's harlots aren't slaves," Doris said.

"Yes they are. Didn't you see the sadness in their eyes? Couldn't you tell that their spirits were broken?"

"I thought they were pretty," Doris said.

"Pretty, yes, but they showed no emotions. They've got no feeling for life, no joy in their hearts. What have they got to live for? Work, work, and then more work, Where's the fun? Where's the happiness?"

"I think you're being a little too dramatic, Bolt," said Abby.

"I'm just trying to make a point. Here you have fun together. You're a family. You eat together and garden together, laugh together. You can go to Harmony if you're troubled. Or me, or Tom."

"We've heard all that," Doris said quietly. "We'll miss all of you, but we've made our decision. You can talk until your throat is parched and it won't do any good."

"I'm not trying to tell you what to do, but I don't think you'll be very happy over there. At least here, you can be by yourself if you want to be. You can ride off in the country or go to town. What'll it be like over there? You won't have any time for pleasure. Hell, you'll probably never seen San Antonio again. You'll be trapped at that damned whorehouse.

"No, we won't," said Abby. "Jessie said we could go anywhere we wanted to."

"Sure, but when will you have time if you're working eighteen hours a day?" Bolt picked up one of the pillows and slammed it back down on the bed.

"It won't be that bad," said Doris.

"Did you ask where you'll sleep over there?"

"No."

"Here you've got your own upstairs bedrooms," he gestured, "away from the cottages out back where you take the men. My guess is that over at The Proud Peacock, you'll have to sleep in the cribs where you work. You'll sleep on dirty sheets and you'll have to live with the constant stench of sweat and the musk of lovemaking."

"Bolt, please, you're only making it harder on all of us," Doris said.

"I'm just worried about you. I don't trust Jessie at all. She's viciously cruel and evil. I know there's something strange going on over there at The Proud Peacock, something very bad, and I don't want you two to get hurt."

"Jessie told us you'd react this way," Abby said, with a hint of sarcasm to her voice. "I still say it's sour grapes."

Bolt threw his hands in the air. "I give up. You girls do what you want to. Just remember, you've got a home here if you want it. If things get too rough over there, you can come back."

"Thanks for everything, Bolt," Doris said. She didn't look him in the eye. She folded her hands together and stared down at them.

Bolt thought she saw tears in her eyes just before she lowered her head, but he couldn't be sure. He sighed, already sensing the sadness that would soon envelop them. He walked over and hugged Doris, then gave Abby a brief squeeze.

"I won't say goodbye," he said. "I'll just wish you good luck. I hope you'll be happy because that's all that really matters in life."

He left before his anger erupted again.



Tom was furious when he heard the news later that afternoon.

"But Doris and Abby are two of my favorites," he cried after Bolt told him about the girls when he got back from town.

"We can't force them to stay," Bolt said, finally accepting the girls' decision.

"So Jessie sweet-talked them into it, the phony bitch."

"That's about it," Bolt said.

"If they want to go over to the enemy, I say let 'em go, the disloyal sluts."

"Don't be too hard on them, Tom. The girls are confused, that's all."

"That's all?" Tom raged.

"We can't do anything about it, Tom. We've all tried."

"Why don't you match Jessie's offer? Or better it?" Tom suggested.

"I've considered it, but I've decided against such tactics. I'm not going to play Jessie's game.

I'm not a pimp. We give fair wages to gals who choose this kind of life. We let 'em go their own way. We won't tempt them with better offers."

"But, this Jezebel bitch is screwing you and you don't even get a kiss."

Bolt shrugged. "It may work out."

"If you think so, Bolt, you're more naive than the girls."

# CHAPTER SIX

Bolt got mad every time he rode to town, and he rode to town every day to see if he could learn anything new about Jessie Belle, or The Proud Peacock. He passed Jessie's whorehouse sign coming and going, and that's all it took to set him off again.

"I'm getting worried, Tom," Bolt said as he took a sip of warm beer.

It was Sunday, late afternoon, and the two of them sat at a small table in the Rusty Nail Saloon in San Antonio, two miles away from the Rocking Bar Ranch. Being a Sunday, there were only three other customers in the saloon that time of day, and Bolt welcomed the quiet.

A half-full pitcher of beer sat on the table between them. Their broken-in Stetsons were on the table, too, set off to the side.

Bolt had been restless out at the ranch, mostly because it was the day of the week he and Tom usually spent with Harmony and the girls. When Bolt had suggested they ride into town, Tom had jumped at the chance.

"You can't let it eat at you this way," Tom said. "It's all you ever think about."

"It's been a week now and we haven't heard a peep from Doris and Abby. I thought for sure they'd be back home by now."

"Maybe they like it over there at Jezebel's whorehouse. Quit worrying about them."

"It isn't only that, Tom. Business at our bordello has dropped off to almost nothing this past week. Hell, we're lucky if we have one or two customers a night."

"I know. Friday and Saturday nights have always been our busy nights. How many fellows were there last night? Three?"

Bolt shook his head. "No, that was Friday night. Last night we only had one lonely customer. Even our regulars are going over to Jessie's place."

"Well, it's no wonder she's getting all the business. She's got flyers tacked up all over town. Hell, every time we go into a saloon, the fellers are all talking about the naughty girls Jessie has at The Proud Peacock."

Bolt sighed. "Jessie might have called it right when she said she'd put us out of business within a week."

"Business will pick up again after the novelty of Jezebel's whorehouse wears off."

"I hope so," Bolt said.

"If I didn't hate Jezebel so much, I'd be tempted to ride over there and see for myself just how naughty her girls are," Tom grinned.

"If my hunch is right, Jessie's got those girls performing all sorts of sick sexual acts just to keep the customers coming back."

"You're probably right."

"I just hope there aren't too many men who got their sexual thrills by beating the girls half to death. I just couldn't stand it if the girls were being tortured." He shuddered at thought of it.

"They'd be back at the ranch if things got too rough for them, so quit worrying about it."

The straightback chair squeaked when Bolt leaned back in it. He picked up his Stetson, turned it slowly in his hands.

"You know, Tom, it might not be a bad idea if you went to The Proud Peacock after all."

"No thank you," Tom said firmly. "I can't stomach that Jezebel. I'd probably punch her out and end up dead of strangulation at the hands of Brutus. I know when to let well enough alone."

"You said you wanted to climb the bones of one of those tall Spanish whores."

"I don't want it bad enough to die for it."

"Aw, come on, Tom. You're too much of a gentleman to hit a lady."

"I am, but she's no lady."

"You might be missing something great if you pass up the chance," Bolt urged. "You've heard the fellows rave about them. Those whores must have something special going for them."

"I don't aim to find out what it is."

A frown creased Bolt's forehead. He gave his Stetson a final twirl and set it back down on the table as he sat up straight.

"I give up," he sighed. "You're a stubborn old cuss."

"Yep." Tom grinned and took a sip of beer.

Neither one of them spoke after that. They'd exhausted that line of conversation.

Bolt glanced over when he heard the batwing doors swing open. Two scruffy looking men entered the room and marched straight to the long bar across the room from where Tom and Bolt sat.

"Double whiskey," the shorter of the two men said to the barkeep.

"Same here, Bill," said the other man.

"Let's see," said the barkeep. "You're Charlie, and you're Wade."

"That's right," laughed the shorter customer. "I'm Wade and this is my partner, Charlie."

"You got a damned good memory," said the one named Charlie. "We was only in here long enough for one drink last night."

Bolt was always amazed at Bill's memory. He'd seen him recall a stranger's name more than once.

"Did you fellows ever get paid for those cattle you herded in here yesterday?" Bill asked as he poured the drinks and slid them across the bar.

"Not yet," Charlie said. "We was waitin' around out at the stockyard this mornin' when we found out the buyer won't be in till tomorrow. Seems his horse broke a leg yesterday, way north of here, and he had to shoot the poor animal."

"Yeah," said Wade. "Then Joe Lacato, he's the buyer, he was stuck out in the middle of nowhere. Poor fellow had to walk four or five miles in the boiling hot sun before another rider happened along."

"Lucky for Lacato this Madonna kid came

along when he did," Charlie interjected. "Lacato was staggering around in circles when Mike Madonna found him out there. Madonna probably saved the old man's life."

"That he did," Wade said. "The sun was frying the old fellow's brains out. Madonna gave him a ride to the next town so's Lacato could buy another horse."

"How'd you find out?" Bill asked as he wiped the counter with a stained bar towel.

"Madonna delivered the message to us out to the stockyard this morning," said Charlie. "He said the buyer was so tired, he was gonna spend the night in that there town before he started out again."

Bolt listened to the men talk, just because it took his mind off his own problems. He liked Bill, the barkeep, who was a round, roly-poly fellow, good-natured as hell. Bill drank too much of his own home brew for his own good. He never got drunk, but it all went straight to his gut.

"Lacato had better show up tomorrow," Charlie laughed. "Me and Wade are down to our last two nickels."

"Too bad about the delay," Bill said. "If I remember right, you fellows wanted to start out for home today."

"We sure did, but it's workin' out," said Wade. He paused long enough to down his drink. "In fact, we ran into some good luck along the way."

"How's that?" Bill asked.

"There was this real friendly sort out at the stockyard this mornin'," Wade said, "and when he

76

learned of our situation, he told us about a whore-house where we could pass the time of day."

Bolt's interest perked up and he found himself straining to hear every word of the conversation. By the way Tom was staring blankly into his glass of beer, he know Tom was listening, too.

"Beats the hell out of sittin' in the hot sun all day," Bill said.

"Sure does," said Charlie. "And the feller even offered to ride out there to the whorehouse with us so's we didn't get lost." He raised his glass and downed the double shot of whiskey in one gulp.

"Lucky you," Bill commented. He poured more whiskey in the two empty glasses.

"Oh, that weren't the lucky part of it," said Wade. "We told that there stranger that we was flat busted until our buyer showed up. Hell, after payin' for a room and a meal and a couple of drinks last night, we didn't even have a half-dollar between us for a haircut and a stinkin' bath."

Bolt wondered how in the hell they were gong to pay for their drinks if they didn't even have enough money for a bath.

"That's a tough position to be in," Bill laughed. "You got paradise right there in your sights and no way to pop your pistol."

"Wait, I ain't through," said Wade. "This stran-ger feller, he says it don't matter that we're busted. We could go to the whorehouse for free."

"Is that right?" the barkeep said.

"Yep. He told us we could have our pick of the whores and whatever we wanted in the way of drink while we was there," Charlie added. "And all

77

for free. We was dumbfounded."

"I wonder why the stranger was so generous," Bill said.

"Seems the whorehouse is new and they're wantin' to drum up some business."

"Well, they must be mighty damned desperate for customers if they'd let the likes of you two in," Bill laughed.

"They wasn't needin' any more customers. Not as far as I could tell," Charlie said. "We was there at high noon and had to wait more than an hour for a whore."

Bolt and Tom exchanged worried glances. Bolt shrugged his shoulders, took a sip of beer and set his glass back down on the table.

"I'll be damned," Bill said.

"It's true," said Charlie, "And they kept offering us those free drinks while we was waitin'. It was mighty tempting, but I don't drink nothin' harder than water before three o'clock of an afternoon. We didn't drink any of their whiskey, but we still got our money's worth. Huh, Wade?" Charlie laughed heartily and slapped his partner on the back.

"We sure as hell did," Wade said. "The madam out there, this Miss Jezebel, now ain't that a name for ya? Well, I think she took a fancy to Charlie and me. Anyways she paid more attention to us than she did to any of the other fellers out there. She kept insistin' that we have a drink, didn't she, Charlie?"

"Yeah. That little redhead don't take no for an answer. I reckon we offended her by refusin' her hospitality."

"We just had to keep tellin' her we didn't want any liquor," Wade chuckled. "Now, I ain't like old Charlie, here. I don't care what time a day it is when I do my drinkin', but I never touch the stuff before I go to bed with a woman."

"How odd," Bill said.

Wade leaned toward the barkeep and spoke in a hushed voice. "I sure as hell didn't want to tell Miss Jezebel this, but after a couple of stiff drinks, my pecker goes limp as a noodle. Happens every damned time. I ain't about to embarrass myself like that in front of a whore, so I just leave the booze alone till I'm all through."

"That ain't so bad," the barkeep said. "My pecker problem is even worse than that."

"Oh, I'm sorry," said Wade sincerely. "What's your trouble?"

"Hell," said Bill, "with this big gut, I can't even find the damned thing when I need it."

All three men laughed so hard their faces turned red.

"Corny," Tom said.

"Yeah," Bolt agreed. "I've heard Bill pull that one before. He knows how to sucker them in."

"We'll have one more drink," said Wade, "and then we got to go rent us a room for the night."

Bill filled their tumblers again. "You fellers can settle up with me in the mornin' after you get your pay. I ain't worried about it. But you might have trouble getting a room on credit. Too many drifters come through town, too many drovers."

A wide grin broke across Wade's face. He dug

79

down into his pocket and drew out a paper bill, and waved it in the air.

"We don't work that way, Bill," he said. "We pay as we go. We don't owe nobody nothin' and we're gonna keep it that way. You didn't think we'd order drinks if we couldn't pay for 'em, did you?"

"It wouldn't have mattered. What'd you do, steal money from one of the whores?" Bill laughed.

"Nope," said Wade. "That feller what brought us out to the whorehouse, think his name was Phil Rawley or somethin' like that. Well, anyways, damned if he didn't slip each of us a ten-dollar bill as we was fixin' to leave."

"You fellows have all the luck," Bill said.

"The Rawley feller told us to tell all of our friends, and all the drovers we saw, about how good The Proud Peacock is. He's wantin' us to do his advertising for him."

"So, are you gonna spread the word for him?" Bill asked.

"Hell, no," said Charlie. "We ain't no damned pimps."

Bolt snickered and covered his mouth. "You know, I like those fellows," he said.

"Me, too. You want more beer?" Tom hoisted the still half-full pitcher.

"No, I'm getting restless. I'm ready to go if you are."

"I'm ready."

Bolt picked up the pitcher of beer, carried it over to the bar. He pulled a five-dollar gold piece out of his picket and plunked it on the counter.

"You gentlemen leaving so soon?" Bill asked.

"Yep. Thanks, Bill. And buy these nice gentlemen a couple of drinks, will you?" He grinned at Bill and Bill gave him a knowing nod.

"Well, thank you, sir," Wade said, a puzzled look on his face.

Bolt tipped his hat and headed for the batwing doors with Tom at his side.

"Looks like your luck is still holding, fellows. Have another drink," Bill said to the two drovers as Bolt and Tom walked out into the brightness of the late afternoon sun.

"Why in the hell didn't you tell them who we were?" Tom said when they got outside.

"I don't need to, Tom." Bolt looked over at his friend and grinned. "Bill will tell them who bought their drinks. And I'll bet my sweet ass that we get more advertising out of Jessie's dirty money than she does."

# CHAPTER SEVEN

The two friends rode along the hot, dusty trail for a long time before either one of them spoke. Bolt tipped his hat back and stared at the sky for a long time. He saw only a few thin clouds and was discouraged. He shook his head and slid his Stetson back in place.

"Well, Bolt, what do you think," Tom finally asked.

"It isn't gonna rain today."

"That ain't what I meant."

"You asked, and that was what I was thinking at the moment. I can't read your mind."

"And I can't read yours either, Bolt, unless you want to say it out loud." Tom spoke with an edge of sarcasm to his voice. "You know damned well I was talking about Jezebel and The Proud Peacock."

"Yeah, I guess we're both edgy today. I really don't know what to think, Tom. I've been running things through my mind ever since we left the saloon."

"So have I, but none of it makes sense."

"I know what you mean. It seems like we learned a lot by listening to those cattle drovers, and yet, when I think it all through, I come up with the same result. I don't think we learned a damned thing we didn't already know."

"Maybe if we do our thinking out loud, we can put the pieces of the puzzle together," Tom suggested.

"All right. You start."

"Well, we learned that Jessie Belle is so desperate to lure new customers into her whorehouse, that she's willing to let some men have a piece of ass for free in exchange for them passing the word along."

"On the other hand, the drovers said she had so many customers, they had to wait in line." Bolt thought for a moment. "If Jessie had a lot of paying customers, why would she need to drag men off the trail, so to speak?"

"I don't know. To spread the word about The Proud Peacock, I guess. That's what those drovers said anyway."

"Then she must be trying to lure every damned man in San Antonio out to her bordello."

"It must be working," Tom said. "We sure as hell haven't had any business this past week."

"I can see her trying to attract the townsmen who might become regular customers, but why would she bother with the drifters, the drovers?"

"Maybe she figures they'll talk to other drovers along the trail and spread the word across the whole wide West," Tom reasoned.

"Hell, she couldn't handle all of them if they showed up at her doorstep. She's crazy."

"Maybe she's planning to expand and take over

all of Cow Town."

"Well, she's got more ambition than I do," Bolt laughed. "I'm satisfied with the small, steady stream of customers who come our way."

"What else do we know?" Tom said.

"We know that one of the drovers gets a limp dick if he drinks too much. Therefore, he doesn't drink before he screws."

"And the other fellow doesn't drink until three of an afternoon," Tom laughed. "And who really cares?"

"Not me." Bolt sat up taller in the saddle, flexed his stiffening muscles.

"Then I think we can forget about the fact that neither one of the drovers drank while they were at The Proud Peacock."

"I agree," Bolt said. "It doesn't seem to make any difference."

"We know that the drovers' names are Charlie and Wade and that they drink whiskey, but that doesn't matter either."

"Nope. Not a damned thing."

"Why would Jessie keep offering them drinks if they told her they didn't want any?" Tom asked.

"To prove to everyone that she's got a classy whorehouse, I reckon. Extra trimmings. Like those gawdawful gold rope sashes she's got tacked up all over her place."

"Oh, those are hideous. How in the hell does Jessie expect to make any money if she's giving away free drinks?"

"A couple of drinks aren't going to bust her. I'm sure she doesn't do that very often. In fact, I'll bet she charges everyone else a pretty penny."

"I wonder how much she charges for her whores?" Tom said.

"Why don't you stop on the way back and find out?" Bolt said.

"Nope. I'm not that curious."

"Well, as far as figuring this thing out, I'd say we're right back where we started. Nowhere."

"Then maybe we should forget about the whole damned thing," Tom said. "Jessie's gonna do what she's gonna do, and I don't think our lives should have to revolve around her."

Bolt wasn't listening. He was still thinking.

"Tom," he said, "don't you think it was odd that Charlie and Wade just happened to meet up with one of Jessie's men at the stockyard this morning?"

"You mean the stranger, Phil Rawley, I think they said, who took them out to The Proud Peacock and then slipped them twenty dollars when they left?"

"Yes. It seems like more than just a coincidence to me. In fact, the way I figure it, Charlie and Wade weren't having a streak of good luck. Jessie's man was there waiting for them. Or maybe he was waiting for any poor drover who was down on his luck."

"Doesn't seem odd to me. Jessie's trying to build up her business. What better place to find lonely, horny men than at the stockyard? Hell, most of those fellows haven't seen a woman for two or three months. You should remember what it was like when we were herding cattle."

"I do. I say we forget about it. Even if business falls off at the bordello for awhile, we've still got the cattle."

"Good idea, Bolt. Good idea." Tom started whistling.

Anxious to get home, Bolt picked up the pace of his horse. Tom did the same to his horse and fell in line behind Bolt.

Bolt closed his eyes, tipped his head up and basked in the warm breeze that floated across his face. He drew in a slow, deep breath and smelled the earth and the grasses, the strong horseflesh. He listened to the sound of the horses' hoofbeats, and imagined himself on the open trails again. For a few minutes he let the peace and serenity of the countryside settle over him like a protective shroud.

When he opened his eyes again, the feeling of solitude was snatched away from him as if a big wind had come and blown it away. Up the road a piece, the sign that marked The Proud Peacock stuck out like a boil on an elephant's butt.

"Well, there it is," said Tom, who now rode beside him. "Shall we shoot it full of holes?"

"Why waste the ammunition?"

"Yair, but it's sure tempting."

"Tom, you really should stop at The Proud Peacock for a spell as long as we're right here. You could put the boots to one of Jessie's whores and you could check on Doris and Abby while you're there."

"No," Tom said stubbornly. "Go on in there yourself if you're so damned curious."

"I can't do that, Tom. If I went in there, it would give Jessie all the ammunition she needs to prove to Doris and Abby that I'm trying to run their lives. You've got a reason for going there. Jessie wouldn't think anything about it. For crissakes, I'm askin' a favor of you, Tom."

Tom shook his head vigorously. "No, sir, my friend. Not this time. I've done favors for you before and nearly gotten killed for my trouble."

"Thanks a lot, Tom," Bolt said sarcastically.

"And would you quit your damned stewing about Doris and Abby. They were the ones who made the decision to work at The Proud Peacock, so let 'em do it. You're not responsible for them anymore."

"You're right, Tom, but it's hard to let go when you know they might be in danger."

"Hell, they cooked their own beans and now they can eat 'em. If they end up fartin', it's their own damned fault."

By the time they turned onto the Rocking Bar Ranch path a few minutes later, Bolt was filled with a shadowy feeling of elation. He had accepted the fact that while he'd done as much for Doris and Abby as he could possibly do, they were now on their own to seek their own positions in life.

The sun was gone now and the gray shroud of evening settled over the land. It was almost suppertime, and Bolt was starved.

He looked forward to Harmony's special chicken and dumplings, which she cooked almost every Sunday evening. He hoped Linda Ramsey,

Cathy Boring, and the other two harlots, Winny Hart and Doreen Jenson, would be at the supper table tonight, as they usually were on Sundays. It was the one night of the week when all of them got together for a meal in the big ranch house.

Tom offered to feed and water their two horses before supper, so after Bolt put Nick in the stable, he walked on up to the house.

The house seemed unusually quiet when he opened the back door and glanced inside. When he stepped through the door, he realized that there was no aroma of mealtime preparations. No lanterns burning and flickering to light the darkening rooms. No sounds of kitchen utensils clattering, nor of Harmony puttering around the house.

Shards of panic pierced his heart and made his throat go dry. An instant later, a wave of relief washed over him. The smells of chicken cooking and bread fresh from the oven had come to him earlier, when he had started up the hill. He knew then that, for some reason, Harmony had cooked their Sunday supper in the kitchen of the living quarters at the bordello down the hill.

He went back outside and closed the door, yelled at Tom on his way down the hill and told him that they would be eating supper at the bordello.

"I'm home," he yelled as he strolled through the door of the large rustic cabin. "And I'm hungry as a bear."

Harmony dashed from the kitchen, wiping her sticky hands on her apron.

"Bolt, I'm glad you're back."

"What's the matter, Harmony?" He saw the quiet look of helplessness in her eyes, the anxiety in her facial expression.

"Abby's back."

"Good," Bolt said, with a sense of relief. "I Knew she wouldn't last very long over there. Where is she?" He scanned the room and didn't see any of the other girls.

"She's upstairs in bed," Harmony said softly. "She's hurting pretty bad."

"What do you mean?" An alarm went off in Bolt's head as his gaze shot to the stairway.

Harmony put her hand on Bolt's arm.

"Abby's been beaten, Bolt," she said as she squeezed his arm. "She's got bruises and welts all over her body."

"I knew it." Bolt said, shaking his head sadly. "I just knew this would happen."

"Abby is very sick right now, Bolt, but she'll be all right in time," Harmony said in a soft, calming voice. "We'll nurse her back in health."

And then Bolt clenched his fists so hard he nearly tore the flesh open with his fingernails.

"I promise you," he said, his eyes full of hatred, "before I'm through, Jessie Belle will be sorry she ever set foot on The Rocking Bar Ranch."

# CHAPTER EIGHT

"Abby's been asking for you, Bolt," Harmony said. "I think you should go up and see her."

"Yes, I want to." Bolt walked across the room, his stride long and full of determination. Beyond the staircase, three of the girls who worked for him, Cathy Boring, Winny Hart and Doreen Jenson, huddled in the doorway of the hall that led to the kitchen. They wore plain, long housedresses and no makeup. The worried expressions on their faces were masked with questioning looks of anticipation, as if Bolt were a knight in shining armor, as if his presence would make everything right again.

Bolt paid little attention to them but paused at the bottom of the steps long enough to regain his composure. He unclenched his fists, forced his shoulder muscles to relax, and tried to rid his mind of the terrible anger that blotted out his ability to think clearly.

"I'll go with you," Harmony said as she turned on her heel and followed after him.

When she came up behind him, Bolt took a deep breath, squared his shoulders, and started up the stairs.

Tom came through the front door just then. He stopped and sniffed the air. "Smells good. How come we're eatin' down here tonight?"

"Abby's back. Some bastard roughed her up," Bolt yelled from half way up the stairs, and felt the tension of rage begin to tauten his muscles again. "Just like I figured would happen, that bitch Jessie is letting the men slap the whores around. The girls will tell you about it." With Harmony right behind him, he dashed on up the steps.

He sensed the graveness of Abby's condition as soon as he entered her quiet, darkened bedroom.

The room smelled of liniments and salve and sickbed tonics. The curtains were closed tight, blocking out the gray of evening. The only light in the room came from the low-burning lantern that sat on the bedside table. Next to the lamp were some sulphur matches and a small brass bell with a wooden handle. On the same table were the medicines, the clean dressings and bandages, and the big porcelain basin, which usually sat on the dresser. The basin was hand-painted with delicate pink roses and held water from the matching pitcher, which was still on the dresser.

Linda Ramsey leaned over the bed, gently dabbing at Abby's face with a damp cloth. She looked around when she heard Bolt come into the room.

"Oh, you're here," said she in a hushed voice.

Bolt walked over and Linda lifted the cloth so he could see Abby's wounds.

Abby was covered with a patchwork quilt and

only her arms and face were left uncovered. Her eyes were closed and the damp ringlets of her light brown hair framed her face. She wore a pink robe and her arms, sheathed by the long sleeves of the robe, rested at her sides on top of the quilt.

"Isn't it awful?" Harmony whispered from behind him.

Bolt's stomach knotted with nausea when he saw the blue-black swelling around her cheekbone, the puffiness of one eye. He saw the scabbed-over cut across her chin and wondered if her chin had been smashed by a brutal fist, or slices open with a Barlow pocketknife.

"Oh, my God, Abby," he said.

Abby opened her eyes and looked up at him. The one eye was just a slit in the mass of swollen, discolored flesh.

"Bolt, I'm sorry," she said, her weak voice no louder than a whisper.

"I know. We all feel bad about this," he said gently. "Are you hurtin' bad?"

"A little."

Bolt saw the pain, the humiliation, in her eyes when she raised her hand slowly and reached out for him. She looked so pathetic, so helpless, he could barely stand to think about the suffering she must have endured. He took her hand in both of his and eased it back down to the guilt.

"Damn, I wish this hadn't happened to you, Abby," he said.

"I . . . I'm scared," she cried. She squeezed his hand as if to hold him there and he felt the lack of strength in her grip.

"I know you are, Abby, but you're home now and you're going to be all right." He placed his free hand on her neck and felt the heat of her fever.

"Will you take care of me?"

"Yes, of course we will, Abby," Bolt said. "Do you want me to go for the doctor?"

"No. Don't leave me," she begged, her voice weak and trembling.

"She's got other bruises but I don't think any bones are broken," Harmony said quietly. "We checked her over very carefully."

"How bad are the bruises?" Bolt asked.

"Pretty bad," said Linda. "I'll show you." She leaned closer to the sick girl and spoke softly. "We're going to put more salve on your back, Abby."

Abby nodded.

Bolt eased his hands away from Abby's smaller one and stepped back so Linda and Harmony could get closer to the bed.

Linda pulled the quilt down and with Harmony's help, they gently rolled the weak girl over on her side so that Abby's back was to them. Linda raised the back of Abby's robe up and drew it up around her neck.

Bolt saw Abby wince, then stiffen, as Harmony carefully peeled the white cloth dressing away from her back.

Bolt gasped involuntarily when he saw the long red welts on Abby's back. Seven or eight of them, at least. His knees went weak when he thought about how frightened Abby must have been when the wounds had been inflicted on her delicate body. Blood still oozed from those places on several of the raw, raised welts where the skin had been broken.

He stared at Abby's back and couldn't imagine anyone cruel enough, or sick enough, to beat a poor defenseless girl so badly. With a whip, or a long leather thong, he thought, and that went way beyond the occasional slapping around that Jessie Belle said her whores encountered in their work.

The medicinal smell became more pungent when Harmony opened the small jar of salve. She leaned over the bed and carefully applied the salve to the raw wounds. Abby flinched each time Harmony touched her, but she didn't cry out.

As Bolt watched Linda and Harmony tend to Abby's wounds, he struggled to control the anger that raged through him like a fire started somewhere deep in his gut and spreading out of control as it flamed through his mind. He hated the bastard who'd done this to Abby. He hated Jessie Belle even more for allowing it to happen.

Linda fixed a fresh dressing out of a square of the clean cloth and placed it on Abby's back so that it covered all of her wounds. Linda and Harmony worked together to fasten the dressing in place by wrapping two long, narrow strips of the cloth across the dressing and then around Abby's body, tying the strips with small, neat knots.

The two girls slid the back of Abby's robe back down into place, then eased her onto her bruised back. Before they drew the quilt up and tucked it around the sick girl, Harmony pulled the front of Abby's robe back just far enough to expose the top part of one of the girl's breasts. She pointed to a thin, inch-long cut just above the nipple.

Bolt frowned when he studied the small cut. It was red and puffy beneath the scab and looked infected.

Harmony closed the robe and turned away. She tugged at Bolt's shirtsleeve, pulled him to the side. "Some bastard started to carve his initials in Abby's breast," Harmony said, her eyes flashing with bitterness.

Bolt shook his head and again imagined Abby's terror as she was being tortured.

"Does she know who did it?" Bolt asked.

"By sight, but not by name," Harmony said. "It was one of her customers."

"Rough boy."

"You two go on down to supper," Linda said. "I'll stay here with Abby."

"You all go eat," Abby said. "I want to rest for a while."

"Are you sure?" Linda said.

"Yes. I feel safe now that Bolt's here," Abby said in a low voice. Her words were slow and labored, as if it took all of her energy just to say them. She turned her head slightly and tried to smile. She grimaced in pain instead.

"We'll bring you some more broth in a little while," Harmony said. "And ring that bell if you need anything."

Bolt was worried about Abby, but he didn't

want her to know it. He walked to the edge of the bed and smiled down at her. "You get some sleep now, gal," he teased. "I'll be back up here after supper and I might feel like waltzin' you around the room."

"I'd get out of bed for that," Abby said, her voice so weak Bolt had to strain his ears to hear the words. A thin smile played at her lips and then her eyes drooped shut.

"She'll sleep now," Harmony said. "Let's leave her alone."

"I'll be down in a minute," Linda said.

Harmony and Bolt walked out of the room, leaving Linda to tidy up.

"Did Abby tell you what happened?" Bolt asked as they headed for the stairs.

"Yes," Harmony said, her hand floating across the smooth banister as she walked down the steps. "She had a customer last night who got his thrills by hurting her."

"The dirty bastard," Bolt said, his jaw tight. "I'd like to kill him."

"Abby said it was pretty bad over there at The Proud Peacock. It seems Jessie Belle attracts rough customers."

"I already figured that."

"The girls were ordered to do whatever the customers demanded of them, no matter how degrading it was, no matter how painful it was for them. The more weird the sex act they had to perform, the more Jessie charged the customer."

"I know," said Bolt. "I'll bet Jessie made a small fortune off the bastard who fucked Abby up."

"Probably," Harmony said as she reached the bottom step. "It's bad enough the girls have to put up with the sick, brutal men, but the thing that really irks me is that the girls don't get paid any extra for their pain. Abby said that bastard who beat her up last night kept bragging about how he'd paid a hundred dollars for the privilege of inflicting pain on her and he was sure as hell going to get his money's worth."

"A hundred dollars?" Bolt said. "Jessie's worse than the damned men who patronize her whorehouse." The others were in the kitchen when he and Harmony got downstairs, so Bolt paused long enough to hear what Harmony had to say.

"Abby said it wasn't too bad at first. She said the type of men who came to The Proud Peacock were a lot rougher than the ones we get here, but she could handle it. They pushed her around a little and slapped her if she balked at some of their demands. She said she learned real quick that it was easier to do whatever the customers wanted."

Bolt cupped his hand over his chin and stared down at the floor. "It ain't right. No woman should be treated like that."

"She had one customer who treated her decently, at least," Harmony said. "A drifter who came to town looking for a job. He promised Abby he'd come back the following night, but she never saw him again."

"And I'll bet he didn't have to pay for the services of a whore."

"Or for his drinks," Linda Ramsey said as she

came down the steps. "Abby told me she was glad this fellow was a happy drunk. Apparently he was offered all the free drinks he wanted while he waited for a whore, and by the time he got his turn with Abby, he was a little tipsy."

"Too bad all the men weren't like that," Bolt said. "It makes me sick to think about Abby, and now I'm wondering about Doris."

"Abby said she tried to get Doris to come home with her," Harmony said, "but Doris wouldn't come. She still thinks she can make a lot of money."

"What good will it do her if she ends up crippled or dead?" Bolt said dryly.

"I guess Jessie Belle's determined to herd the men in over there like cattle at roundup time," Linda said. "Abby says she's spent more time on her back in the past week than she's spent sitting or standing up. Sixteen hours a day."

"Jessie's a greedy bitch," Bolt said.

"Did Harmony tell you about the bastard who whipped Abby?"

"Only that he was a customer and he paid a hundred dollars for the sport," Bolt said.

"Well," said Linda, "the vicous pervert tied her to the bed, spread-eagle, face down, and then kept yelling, 'You will submit to me, you dog-faced bitch.' Abby said she just gritted her teeth and prayed it would be over with, but the dirty swine kept yelling the same thing and striking her with a whip every time he said it."

"And when he was through with her," Harmony said, "the filthy pig turned her over on her back

98

and tied her up again and then started to carve his initials into the flesh of Abby's breast."

"He said he wanted to brand her so everybody knew she was his," added Linda.

"And he said he'd come back and finish carving his initials another time so she'd have something to look forward to," Harmony said.

"The sonofabitch," Bolt said as the anger raced through him again. He clenched his fists without even knowing he'd done it.

"I can't bear to think about it any more," Linda said with a shiver. "It must have been just terrible for Abby."

"When did Abby get home?" Bolt asked.

"Shortly after you and Tom left for town this afternoon," Harmony said.

"I'm surprised Jessie would let her go," Bolt said. "Especially with her looking like she does."

"Poor Abby," Linda said, shaking her head sadly. "She said she was so sick after that swine whipped her that she went to Jessie and begged her to have someone bring her back over here."

"Of course Jessie refused," Bolt said.

"Yes. Jessie claimed she couldn't spare any of her men that long. She told Abby she was free to leave but that she'd have to find her own way home because she didn't have any spare horses."

"So did Abby walk home?"

"Yes," said Linda. "Abby said she left at dawn this morning, before Jessie had a chance to change her mind about her leaving. Abby cut through the back forty and she was so weak, it took her until after noon to literally drag herself over here. She looked half dead when we found her outside the bordello."

"Jessie Belle will pay for this," Bolt said with a cold hard edge to his words.

Harmony brushed the wrinkles out of her apron and started toward the kitchen. "It's a sickness, isn't it?" she said, thinking out loud.

"What's that?" Bolt asked.

"Greed, the horrible hunger for power."

"Yes, it's an illness, Harmony, and it's destroyed a lot of decent people."

"It seems to me that Jessie Belle, in her quest for power, is so afraid that you'll get a little business that she's willing to take in any fellow she can find, whether he can pay or not, just to keep him away from the Rocking Bar Bordello."

"I think there's more to it than just greed or lust for power, Harmony," Bolt said as he followed Harmony toward the kitchen. "But I can't put my finger on it. Not yet."

"Bolt," Linda Ramsey called.

Bolt stopped and turned around. He saw Linda still standing in the middle of the living room, a dazed look on her face.

"What is it, Linda?"

"I'm going over there and take care of Jessie Belle and that bastard who hurt Abby."

Bolt walked back over and put his hand on Linda's shoulder. He wondered if she'd gone suddenly crazy with the emotional strain on seeing Abby in such tough condition.

"No, Linda, you might get hurt," Bolt said in a soft, calming voice. "You're going to stay right

100

here. Tom and I'll take care of it."

Linda went on as if she hadn't heard Bolt. "And then I'm going to find Doris and get her out of there before she gets killed."

"No, you can't go over there, Linda," Bolt said. firmly.

Linda looked directly into his eyes and Bolt was frightened by the hatred he saw there.

"You can't stop me, Bolt."

# CHAPTER NINE

Abby Mason seemed to rally the following day and Bolt was relieved. Although she said her back still pained her a lot and her bruised eye felt like it was being pierced by an ice pick whenever she moved, Abby forced herself to get out of bed a couple of times during the day so she could gain back her strength. With Linda supporting her on one side and Harmony on the other, Abby walked slowly around her darkened bedroom, then eased back into bed.

Then the morning after that, Tuesday morning, which was the third day after she'd been whipped and beaten, Abby took a turn for the worse. Her temperature soared to a dangerous level and she suffered the delirium of a high fever.

Tuesday and Wednesday were Abby's worst days and Linda and Harmony spent most of their time at Abby's bedside. Linda was so busy tending to the sick girl that Bolt assumed she'd forgotten about her vow to go over to The Proud Peacock and settle the score with Jessie Belle and the brutal beast who had maimed Abby, if she could even find out who it was. At least Linda never mentioned it.

The other harlots spent a lot of time with Abby, too, which was good for them, Bolt thought. Only one customer visited the bordello during that time, and the harlots didn't have much to do. The customer was Clem Atkins, a grizzled old cowhand from a nearby cattle ranch, who rode over to be pleasured every Monday evening, come rain or come shine. After Monday night, there were no customers at all and Bolt knew the girls were beginning to get edgy about it.

The girls took turns reading books to Abby when she was awake. They helped Harmony and Linda all they could by applying cool, damp cloths to Abby's forehead to bring the awful fever down, and by encouraging her to get better. And when they were away from Abby, they talked among themselves and wondered what the future held for them.

Bolt stayed close to home while Abby was so sick. Unable to concentrate on anything but Abby's precarious condition, he puttered around the house, fixing things that needed attention. He straightened up the stable, and brushed the horses more than they needed to be brushed. And whenever he thought about Abby, his resentment toward Jessie Belle grew to full-blown hatred for the greedy bitch who had allowed this to happen to Abby. And the more he thought about it, the more he was convinced that Jessie encouraged such brutal behavior by her crude male customers just so she could extract bigger fees for the services the whores provided.

Continuously nervous and increasingly jumpy over Abby's condition on Tuesday, and again on Wednesday, Bolt wandered in and out of her upstairs bedroom several times each day. He always found a hushed bustle of activity around Abby's bed as Harmony and Linda fought to bring Abby's temperature down. They kept damp cloths on her forehead and gave her strong doses of foul-smelling tonic. At times, they stripped Abby's robe back away from her bruised body and covered her bare flesh with cool, damp towels. And whenever Abby would begin to shiver with a chill, Harmony and Linda would patiently and lovingly dry Abby's skin and cover her with the patchwork quilt and then layer two more blankets on top of her quilt.

During those times when Abby was awake, Bolt sat by her bedside and talked to her, keeping the conversation light-hearted and yet encouraging her to get well, reminding her that he still wanted to waltz her around the room. She broke his heart at other times when the fever seemed to consume her mind and she ranted deliriously, like a crazed old woman. The worst times for Bolt, though, were when Abby was asleep and he sat back in the hard, straight-backed chair beside her bed and stared at her battered, swollen face, her still, lifeless body, and wondered if she'd make it.

Each time he entered Abby's sick room and smelled the liniments and tonics as he looked down at her bruised face, and her puffy eye where the blue-black flesh was turning a hideous yellow, he couldn't help but think about Jessie Belle and the horribly cruel men she entertained at The Proud Peacock, all at the expense of the whores. As the days passed slowly, Bolt came to loathe the haughty red-headed woman who, despite her diminutive size, thought she was big enough to put him out of business and then have the whole world flock to her doorstep.

Harmony still did the cooking for all of them during Abby's critically sick days, but she refused to leave the bordello house, even for ten minutes. So Bolt and Tom gladly ate their meals down there with the girls, preferring that alternative to eating their own cooking.

When Abby didn't show any improvement by late Wednesday evening, the strain was beginning to show on all of them.

The girls, Cathy, Winny and Doreen, put on forced smiles and presented overly-cheerful attitudes when they visited Abby's room, and then, when they got away from Abby, they moped around the house with long, sad faces. They bickered among themselves over silly little things that didn't matter, and broke into tears with little provocation.

Linda and Harmony found themselves barking orders at each other in front of Abby, and when they realized what they were doing, they clammed up tight and didn't say another word to each other while they were in her room.

Tom stayed away from the house most of the time and Bolt faulted him for not caring about Abby. However, on the rare occasions when Tom visited Abby, Bolt could tell by the serious expression on Tom's face, that he cared very much about Abby's welfare.

Bolt considered himself the type who remained calm and clear-thinking in the face of such grave situations, but he was beginning to feel the tension build up in him, too. He tried to keep his worries to himself and in so doing, he became irritable and had to keep his mouth shut so he wouldn't jump down someone's throat over some trivial annoyance.

Tempers flared after a late supper that evening. Bolt had gone upstairs right before supper to check on Abby and came away with the feeling that she was sinking fast.

Abby was asleep when he walked into her room and Cathy Boring, who was dressed in her tight, scant harlot outfit, was standing next to the bed. Harmony and Linda were near the dresser, talking in whispers to each other. Cathy, her face masked with heavy makeup, stood perfectly still and stared down at Abby for a long time before she turned and walked out of the room without uttering a word.

Bolt waited near the doorway until Cathy was gone and then he strolled over to the bed. Even though Abby was asleep, he talked to her, called her name several times. He became alarmed when Abby didn't wake up or respond to his voice as she had always done before. He placed his hand gently on the side of her neck and felt the damp heat of her high temperature. Although he was relieved to feel a weak pulse, he knew that the fever was still ravaging her body.

As Cathy had done before him, Bolt stood there and stared at Abby for a long time. He watched the quilt rise and fall with her shallow breathing, and wondered how long she would last. He stood there, unaware of the others in the room, until Harmony and Linda came and led him downstairs to eat the late meal.

Supper consisted of cold roast beef, bread and butter, and soup made from the leftover broth and vegetables of the noon meal. Harmony had been too busy to cook anything else. The food was good, but nobody seemed to notice as they sat around the table with somber faces. Nobody spoke during supper, which seemed to add to the air of tension in the room. It was as if they all knew what the others were thinking: that Abby Mason was gravely ill and probably wouldn't live through the night.

"It's the fever that's killing her, you know," Cathy Boring blurted out after she finished the last bite of her food and pushed her plate away.

"Don't say that she's going to die because she isn't," said Doreen Jenson, the tallest of the harlots, and probably the most sensitive.

"Well, she is going to die, and everybody here knows it," Cathy retorted with that arrogant tilt of her head that showed everyone she knew what she was talking about. "Everybody else is just afraid to say it out loud."

It was after nine o'clock and Cathy was the only one of the harlots who wore her skimpy working clothes, "just in case we have some customers tonight," she had said earlier. The other girls had given up hope and wore plain, high-collared, long-skirted dresses and looked as proper as ministers' wives.

Winny Hart sat up straight and brushed a lock of her dark brown hair away from her face. "You shouldn't say things like that, Cathy," she said.

"Why not? Are you superstitious, Win?" Cathy said sarcastically. "You think because I said it, it's going to make it true? Well, it's true anyway."

Bolt pushed his plate aside and leaned back in his chair. He didn't like to interfere with the girls' conversations, but this time he was tempted: He knew that Cathy Boring was generally unsure of herself and she often spoke out of turn, probably an unintentional effort to draw attention to herself, Bolt figured. But tonight, under the circumstances, he could tell that she was upsetting the other girls. Especially Harmony, whose long blond hair was damp and stringy from working so hard to save Abby, and Linda Ramsey, who looked tired beyond description from her all-night vigils at Abby's bedside.

"That isn't what I meant, Cathy," Winny said. "You've got no right to do our thinking for us. Besides, Abby's healing up nicely and she's going to be all right."

"Win's right, Cathy," Doreen said in a gentler tone of voice than Winny had used. "Abby's on the mend. The swelling around her eye is going down and the black and blue bruise around her eye is fading. In fact, all of her injuries are much better."

"Maybe so," said Cathy. "Maybe her bruises and welts are healing, but that fever is eating her up. Just look at the poor girl."

Harmony, who sat on Cathy's left, looked over at the raving girl. "Cathy, we're doing everything we can to bring Abby's temperature down," she said with a great deal of patience.

"Well, maybe it's not enough," Cathy snapped.

"And what do you suggest, Miss Know-It-All?" Linda said as she sat forward and glared across the table at Cathy.

"If I were taking care of Abby," Cathy said with her nose in the air, "I'd fill the wooden tub with cold water from the stream and set her down in it so the water covered everything but her head."

"Oh, no, Cathy," Harmony said as she turned her head sideways and looked at Cathy. "That would be very dangerous for Abby."

"Why? It would cool her off in a hurry and that's what you've got to do."

"No. If she gets too chilled, she's likely to develop a cold in her chest."

"So? She can get over a cold easy enough," Cathy argued.

"Not in her weakened condition," Harmony said. "If she got a cold now, it would probably kill her."

"No one dies from a simple cold," Cathy said with a mocking smirk.

"Yes they do, Cathy," Harmony said. "If Abby caught cold now, it would probably settle in her lungs and then she'd get the coughing sickness, which, I'm sure you know, is almost always fatal in a person as sick and frail as Abby is right now."

"Well, maybe you'll just have to take that chance," Cathy said snidely. "You've got to do something. Her temperature just keeps going up all the time."

"No, it doesn't," Linda said with conviction. "It hasn't dropped any yet, but it most certainly is not going any higher. I know. I've been with Abby almost all of the time since she came back."

"Are you saying that I haven't spent enough time with Abby?"

Bolt saw that Cathy was on the edge of hysteria. Her voice was harsh and high-pitched, her eyes narrowed to accusing slits. She clutched at the edge of the table as if she were trying to hold on and Bolt had the feeling that if she let go of the table, she'd fall apart completely and erupt in hysterical sobs.

From his position at the head of the table, Bolt glanced around at the other girls and saw that they were also feeling the strain of Abby's illness.

"I'm not saying anything of the kind," Linda said, her face flushed with anger. "You're just a jealous, unfeeling troublemaker."

"Well, at least I'm not pretending to be a doctor

like you and Harmony are," Cathy said, her sarcasm as sharp as a razor.

"We're not pretending anything," Linda huffed. "We're taking care of Abby the best way we know how. And we're doing a hell of a lot of praying, not bitching like you are."

"Well, it isn't enough. Abby needs a doctor," Cathy said. "Plain common sense should tell you that she's burning up. She was even sweating when I was up there a while ago."

"And that's a good sign, Cathy," Harmony said calmly.

"Ha! A lot you know about it."

"As a matter of fact, I do," Harmony said. "I've had a lot of experience with this sort of thing."

"Then why didn't you become a nurse instead a sullied madam?" Cathy yelled.

Bolt saw Harmony's pale cheeks flush crimson as she stared down at the plate. She took a deep breath. He waited for her to explode with anger and let Cathy have it with both barrels. Instead, Harmony lifted her head, looked directly at Cathy, and spoke to her in a gentle voice.

"Look, Cathy, I know just how you're feeling right now, and I want you to know that you're not alone," she said, the compassion showing in her voice. "Hell, we're all edgy right now. We're all scared."

"You are?" Cathy said meekly. "But you all seem so strong."

"No stronger than you are, Cathy," Harmony said. "We're all terribly worried about Abby.

There isn't a one of us here, including Bolt and Tom, I would imagine, who doesn't feel like lashing out at someone or something. We'd all like to yell and pound our fists and blame someone else for Abby's illness."

Bolt nodded at Cathy when she glanced his way. He was grateful that Harmony was clearing the air.

"But it doesn't help Abby any if we bicker among ourselves," Harmony continued. "Abby's alive and she needs our help. She needs our love, our support, our encouragement. She needs our prayers. We all have to pull together. And most of all, we all have to have faith."

Nobody said a word for a minute, then Cathy broke into tears.

"Oh, I've been such a fool," she cried, her shoulders heaving with wracking sobs. "I've just been so worried about Abby, I didn't know what to do."

Harmony reached over and put her arm around Cathy, gave her a squeeze. "Go ahead and cry," she said. "It'll do you good."

"I'm so sorry," Cathy said between sobs.

"Don't worry about it, Cathy," Harmony said. "If I feel the need to cry before this is over, I hope you'll have a shoulder I can lean on."

"I will." Cathy looked up and smiled through her tears. When Harmony withdrew her arm, Cathy dabbed at her eyes with the backs of her hands.

Bolt stood up and sighed. "Thanks, Harmony. I think we all needed that. And quite frankly, I can't think of anybody who gives a better tongue-lashing than you."

"That's not a nice thing to say about me," Harmony said.

Everybody laughed and Bolt felt the tension go out of the room.

Cathy stood up and started to clear the dirty dishes away. "We'll do the dishes so you and Linda can go back upstairs," she said to Harmony.

Doreen and Winny got up to help Cathy as the others walked into the living room. Tom excused himself and went on outside to have a smoke. Bolt walked upstairs with the two girls.

He stood at Abby's bedside and watched her for a long time. Except for her slow, even breathing, she didn't move at all. Not even when he called her name or touched her damp, feverish forehead. He finally turned away.

"I'll sit with her tonight so you girls can get some sleep," he said.

"No, I won't leave Abby," said Harmony.

"Neither will I," said Linda as she started to prepare fresh compresses.

"Besides, you need your beauty sleep," Harmony teased as she escorted Bolt to the doorway. "Now, get out of here."

"That's not a nice thing to say to me," Bolt said, using her very words.

Harmony smiled, but Bolt saw the tears welling up in her eyes.

"Bolt, you'd better go for the doctor first thing in the morning," she said in a hushed voice. "If she lasts that long."

It felt as if a lead ball hit Bolt's stomach as all the frustration and worry and tenseness came crashing back in on him.

"She's that bad?" he asked.

Harmony nodded once, then turned away so Bolt wouldn't see the tears stream down her cheeks.

# CHAPTER TEN

Bolt woke up at dawn Thursday morning, more discouraged about Abby's lack of progress than he'd been since he'd first seen her battered body, four days before.

He slept fitfully during the night, waking often, always thinking that someone had just called his name. Always imagining he heard voices coming from the bordello cabin down the hill. He listened too hard at those times when he awoke with a start, he knew, and even the frogs' croaking began to sound like excited female voices.

And whenever he drifted back into sleep, the bad dreams returned.

Twice during the night, he got up and felt his way through the dark to the kitchen, where he pulled the gingham curtain aside and looked down at the bordello. Both times he saw only the dark shadowy outline of the house down the hill and the pale orange glow of light that shone from one window in the dark house. Abby's room. Where Harmony or Linda, or maybe both girls, would be keeping another all-night vigil at Abby's bedside.

His first thought was of Abby when he awoke

at dawn and he was instantly filled with the same worries and tensions that had been with him constantly for the past few days.

It was a nightmare world he woke up to, a dream world where everything seemed frightening and unreal. He wanted to close his eyes and wake up again and have everything back to normal. And yet, there was something about the early morning that seemed familiar to him. The rain. He heard the rain drops on the roof and that gave him some comfort, some sense of reality. He hoped it was a good omen.

There was something else, too, that seemed vaguely familiar, but he had to concentrate to figure out what it was. He sniffed the air, after testing his other senses. Coffee, he thought. He sniffed again and besides the damp scent of the falling rain, he smelled the heady aroma of freshly brewed coffee, which was something he hadn't smelled in his house in the last few mornings.

Maybe he'd just dreamed that Abby was gravely ill, he thought, as he tried to sort out reality from nightmare in his sleep-fogged mind. But his false sense of security was quickly shattered when he realized that Tom had probably made the coffee this morning. And he sure as hell didn't need Tom's bad coffee to improve his mood.

He slipped into his trousers and walked barefooted into the kitchen, yawning from lack of sleep. He snapped out of his sleepiness when he saw Harmony standing at the counter, her back to him. She was wearing a clean yellow dress.

His heart skipped a beat when he saw her. He

wondered why she was there, and not at Abby's bedside. Oh, no, poor Abby, he thought.

"Is Abby ... did Abby ..." he stammered, not wanting to say what he was thinking.

Harmony whirled around and faced him. His heart beat faster when he saw how tired she looked, how solemn her expression was. He looked into her eyes, searching for some indication of her thoughts.

"Yes," she said with a big sigh. A thin, gentle smile formed on her lips and Bolt saw the tears spring up in her eyes as she was suddenly overcome with emotion.

"Is Abby ... worse?" he asked hesitantly. He felt as if his heart was lodged in his throat, shutting off his breath.

"Abby's fever broke during the night, about midnight. She's going to be all right," she said, her voice trembling as the tears spilled over the brim with the sudden release of pent-up emotions.

"Thank God," Bolt said, and felt his shoulders sag with the rush of relief that flooded through him.

Harmony dashed to him and he grabbed her up in his arms. He felt her soft, pliable body trembling against his and held her for a long time, patting her gently on the back until the sobs subsided.

Harmony finally stepped back away from him. "Look at silly me," she said, laughing through the tears. She dug a clean lace handkerchief out of her bodice pocket and dabbed at her eyes, wiped her nose.

"You deserve a good cry, Harmony. You've been through a hell of a lot in the past few days, and, by God, you pulled her through."

"We all did it," she said.

"You scared the hell out of me when I first saw you," he said with a chuckle. "You looked so tired, so haggard, I thought something had happened to Abby during the night."

"Something did. She woke up," Harmony laughed. "And you'd look wan and haggard, too, if you'd been awake most of the night talking to Abby. When she came out of her deep sleep, she was like a magpie and I thought she'd never shut up."

Tom staggered into the kitchen, rubbing the sleep from his eyes. "It's raining," he mumbled through a yawn. He wore rumpled trousers and without his shirt on, he looked lean and lanky.

"How can you tell? You're still asleep," Bolt said.

"What's going on?" Tom asked, running his fingers through his tousled hair. He squinted against the brightness of the room and looked at Harmony's red-rimmed eyes, her tear-stained face. "Did something happen to Abby?" he asked, suddenly full awake.

"Yes," Harmony smiled. "The crisis has passed, Tom. Abby's much better this morning and she'll be able to outrun you in a day or two."

Tom clenched his fist, punched the air, and let out the loudest "yahoo" Bolt had ever heard.

"Why, Tom, you old soft-hearted sonofabitch,"

Bolt said. "I didn't think you cared about anybody but your rotten old self."

"Don't give me that shit, Mister Big and Brave," Tom said. "I saw that water in your eyes yesterday, and it sure as hell wasn't rainwater."

Harmony fixed them a hearty breakfast and by the time they'd finished eating, the rain had slacked off. While Harmony cleared the dishes away, Bolt and Bolt washed up and put fresh shirts on. The three of them walked down to the bordello, avoiding the puddles and muddy spots, using the wooden steps that Bolt and Tom had built on the slope.

Abby was sitting up in bed when they walked in, pillows propped behind her back. Her long blond hair was shiny clean and freshly curled. The swelling around her eye was almost gone and the purple-yellow bruise had faded even more. Bolt had planned to stay only a few minutes, but Abby was so cheerful and talkative, he found it hard to get away. After an hour, Linda came in and shooed the two men out of the room, declaring that Abby needed to rest.

"I wouldn't have given you a wooden nickel for her life last night," Tom said as he and Bolt walked away from the big rustic cabin.

"I know. I can't believe how good Abby looks this morning," Bolt said.

"It could have gone the other way for her just as easily," Tom said.

"Yes. Another day with that high fever and Abby probably wouldn't have been around to invite us to stay for tea and biscuits."

"I wonder, though," Tom said. "Do you think that fever did something to her brain?"

Bolt frowned. "Why? What do you mean? She seemed all right to me."

"Well, she kept asking you to dance, and that don't sound like the Abby I know."

Bolt laughed. "Don't worry about it, Tom. It was just a little something I promised her if she got better. An incentive."

"You call dancing with you an incentive? Hell, if that's a reward for getting well, you're lucky she's still alive."

"Oh, you think so?"

"Yair. With that kind of an offer to her for getting well, you just cancelled out all the prayers I said for that poor sick girl."

"Better'n goin' to bed with you," Bolt said. "Rumor has it that that's what you offered up for her recovery."

"Yep. Why in the hell do you think she recovered so quickly?" Tom tucked his thumbs into his armpits and grinned like a shit-eating dog. "It wasn't no miracle that snapped her out of it."

"I think it was," Bolt said more seriously. "We'd better get the horses hitched up to the buckboard as soon as we're through with the chores."

Tom gave him a puzzled look. "How come?"

"How else are we going to get the supplies back from town? Carry them on our backs?"

"But it ain't even Monday."

"We didn't go to town last Monday. Remember? We were too worried about Abby."

"Hell, it's too damned muddy to take the wagon

120

to town this morning," Tom said as they walked across the wet grass to the stable.

"The road should dry off some by the time we're ready to go."

"Not that much," Tom said. "What do we need from town that we can't carry in our saddlebags?"

"Grain for the horses, for one thing."

"We've got plenty of grain to last us until next week," Tom said as he glanced up at the dark, hovering clouds. "It's gonna rain again. That road is gonna be a muddy mess all day and I got no hankering to be diggin' the wagon wheels out of a quagmire."

"Then we'll leave the wagon here. It'll be easier that way anyway. I want to go by the stockyards while we're in town."

"Why?" Tom said. "You fixin' to drum up some business for the girls?"

"No. I want to check up on Lyle Watley."

"Watley? You mean Jezebel's henchman? Pretty Boy from The Proud Peacock? The bastard who tried to hustle our guns away from us?"

"Yep."

"What makes you think he'll be at the stockyards?" Tom asked as the two men walked into the stable.

"Just a hunch," Bolt said. "I've been thinking about what those two drovers at the Rusty Nail said about the fellow who offered them free whores at The Proud Peacock. The name they mentioned sounded enough like Lyle Watley to make me curious."

Tom shook his head. "You and your damned

curiosity. Abby's better but you won't give up, will you?"

"Nope." Bolt grinned as he patted his horse on the rump.


"I don't see him anywhere," Bolt said after they had ridden all around the perimeter of the muddy stockyards and were back at the entrance gate. The stench of cow shit was overpowering.

They had already picked up their supplies in town and it was after four o'clock in the afternoon by the time they got to the flat land of the stockyards at the edge of town. The sky was still full of dark, heavy clouds. It had rained again, hard, that morning out at the ranch and Bolt and Tom had delayed their trip to San Antonio until after lunch.

Within the boundaries of the expansive corrals, hundreds of heads of cattle were being herded into huge, separate pens by filthy, weary-looking drovers. Instead of the thunderous roar of hoofbeats, there was the loud plop plop sound of thousands of hooves slogging through the mud.

"Neither do I," said Tom as he eased up on the reins. "But it don't surprise me none. Hell, you don't think Pretty Boy Watley would come out here on a day like this and risk getting himself all wet and dirty, do you?"

"Well, he's missing a bet today. Look at all those poor suckers herding their cattle in from the muddy trail. I'll bet there ain't a one of 'em who wouldn't give a month's pay to crawl into a nice warm body about now."

"We could invite those fellows out to our place," Tom said with a big grin.

"I'm not a pimp, Tom. Besides, I'm not playing Jessie's games."

Bolt reined his horse over to the big, weather-beaten shack near the entrance to the corrals and dismounted. The sign tacked over the door bore the simple legend: OFFICE. The two long wooden benches in front of the shack were still damp from the rain. After he and Tom tied their horses to the hitchrail, where the ground was not so muddy, they walked over and entered the building.

An older fellow, thin and wiry, glanced up from his chair behind the cluttered desk when Bolt and Tom came through the door. He tipped his battered Stetson back on his head and peered over the top of his small, wire-rimmed glasses. He studied them for a minute.

"Good afternoon, gentlemen. I'm Pete Pensor," the clerk said in a raspy voice. "You must be the buyers them fellers were looking for earlier, 'cause you ain't muddy enough to be drovers."

"No," said Bolt. "We're lookin' for someone ourselves."

He glanced around the long room, which was more cluttered and crowded than the clerk's desk. The big, square bulletin board which hung near the door was crammed full of small scraps of paper, messages and notes, and it reminded Bolt of his days as a cattle drover, when he and Tom used similar bulletin boards at other stockyards.

Sometimes the boards had served as a lifeline to a strange city across the West and he and Tom had spent many hours reading the scrawled notes on such boards.

There were crates and barrels stacked all along the walls and the far end of the room was littered with odds and ends of tack and cowboy gear.

"Who you lookin' for?" asked the clerk.

"Lyle Watley. You know him?"

"Yeah, I know Watley." Pete Pensor looked them over again. "I haven't seen him today, but I can tell you where The Proud Peacock is, if that's what you're looking for."

"No," said Bolt. "We're just looking for Watley."

The clerk shrugged his shoulders. "Well, all I can tell you about him is that he's probably out at The Proud Peacock."

"Does he come in here much?" Tom asked.

"Not usually here to my office, but I've seen him hanging around the stockyards a lot the last couple of weeks. Friday, Saturday and Sunday mostly, but he was here Monday of this week, too."

"Thanks," said Bolt as he started to leave.

"Is he a friend of yours?" the clerk asked.

"No," said Bolt.

"I didn't think so," Pensor said. "Well, if I were you, I wouldn't waste my time lookin' him up. I don't much care for that fellow."

"How come, Pete?" Bolt asked.

"He's just a pimp, rounding up customers for that new whorehouse. Nothing wrong with that, I suppose, but he comes around here and bothers

124

the drovers when they're busy bringing in their cattle. And then that slows me down with the paper work I have to do with the drovers."

"Why don't you kick him out?" Tom asked.

The thin clerk shrugged again. "Ain't no law against him bein' here. These stockyards are open to the public. But Watley could do just as well by waiting over at one of the saloons where it don't stink so bad. Hell, first thing every drover does when he's through here at the stockyards is to find a watering hole where he can wash the trail dust out of his throat."

"Yeah, Watley sounds like he's a card short of a full deck," Tom said.

"Well," said Pensor, "if you want to find him, you can go to The Proud Peacock, two miles south of town, or come back in the next couple of days. He'll probably be here."

"Well, thanks for your time, Pete," Bolt said as he turned to leave.

"By the way," the clerk said as Bolt reached for the door handle.

Bolt paused and turned around. "Yair?"

"If you see Watley before I do, tell him that those three fellows he took out to the whorehouse last Monday never came back for their gear."

"Oh?" Bolt said.

"Yeah," said Pensor. "Those fellows were so damned anxious to get to them whores, they asked if they could stow their gear here, saddle-bags and all. They said they'd be back that same night to fetch their gear before they went lookin' for a room, but they never did come back."

"That seems odd," Tom said.

"I thought so, too, but you can see for yourself. The bags are still here." The clerk nodded toward the far end of the room where three sets of saddlebags rested on wooden crates.

"Maybe the men haven't had their fill of the whores," Bolt said with an easy smile.

"Maybe not," said Pensor, "but I'm kind of concerned about it. One of the fellows handed me a small leather pouch and asked me to lock it up in my safe, which I did right while he was standin' there. He said it was his cache of gold and he didn't want to risk having it stolen by one of them whores. I guess I've got an honest face, but I sure as hell don't like to be responsible for other folks' valuables. I got enough to do without worrying about that."

"Then don't worry about it," Bolt said.

"It's been three days, though," the clerk said. "Hell, a man just doesn't leave his gold with a perfect stranger that long, does he?"

"I wouldn't," Tom said. "Not even one with an honest face."

"Not likely we'll be seeing Watley before you do," Bolt said as he opened the office door, "but if we do, Pete, we'll tell him to send those randy men back to town or you're gonna spend all their gold."

"That ain't a bad idea," Pensor laughed.

Bolt and Tom rode straight back to their ranch and got there as the gray skies of the late afternoon were turning even darker with the approaching dusk.

126

They dismounted, walked their horses into the stable and put the animals in their individual stalls, where there was already food and water for them.

"Let's go check on Abby," Bolt said after he finished taking the saddle off Nick and putting it on the barrel where he always kept it.

"Yair," said Tom. "I hope Harmony's got supper ready. I'm starved."

"I just hope we haven't missed supper," Bolt laughed. "It's been a long time since lunch."

Bolt froze in his tracks when he stepped outside the stable. His heart fluttered and seemed to stop in his chest. His breath caught in his throat and he couldn't even speak.

"Shit!" Tom yelled an instant later.

Both men hit the ground at the same time.

# CHAPTER ELEVEN

Bolt instinctively threw his shoulder up and ducked his head behind it as he hit the damp ground. His white Stetson flew off his head and rolled across the damp earth until it came to rest just inside the stable.

The bullet whistled through the air like a rocket, somewhere above his head. Somewhere between him and Tom, who sprawled hatless on the ground nearby, his face buried in the wet dirt, both arms thrown up over his head. Neither of them had had the chance to go for their weapons.

Bolt had seen the woman the instant he stepped out of the stable. She was a shadow of darkness in her flared navy blue skirt, her dark blue scarf over her hair, and the dark shawl around her shoulders. And just before he dove for the ground, he had seen the shiny blur of the pistol in her hand. It was a cheap, nickel-plated pistol, but deadly just the same.

Bolt held his breath, waited for a second shot to be fired. He wanted desperately to roll over on his side so he could get to his gun, but he wasn't in a position to see the woman.

He heard the metal clicking sound of the gun. The suspense was more than he could stand and he could wait no longer. He lowered his shoulder slightly, turned his head just far enough to see the woman.

He saw the dazed look in her wide, pale eyes as the pistol in her small hand wavered back and forth between him and Tom, as if she couldn't decide which one of them to shoot first.

Bolt waited until the woman was staring down at Tom, and then he moved slowly, rolling over on his side. He started to ease his hand down toward his holster, but the movement caught the woman's attention. Her head jerked around and she glared down at Bolt, the pistol suddenly aimed at his head.

"Don't move, mister," the woman screamed. "I'll blow your head off before you can reach it."

Bolt froze when he saw the crazed look in the woman's eyes. Wisps of light-colored hair, gray hair, Bolt thought, stuck out at odd angles from the woman's blue scarf and made her look demented.

He saw the nickel-plated pistol bouncing around as she clutched it in her quivering hand. This was no gun-totin' woman like Jessie Belle, he thought, but who in the hell was this crazy lady who had him pinned to the ground?

"Don't shoot, lady. There's been some mistake," Bolt said as he saw her finger tighten around the trigger. He didn't move a single muscle. He didn't even blink his eyes.

"I am going to kill you." There was a sudden eerie husk to her voice.

Out of the corner of his eye, Bolt saw Tom pulling himself along the ground with his elbows, his hands still clutched over his head. Tom moved slowly, dragging his prone body away from Bolt, and toward a point to the far side of the woman, which would put him out of her line of vision, if he could make it that far before the woman turned on him. Bolt wondered if he could keep her distracted long enough for Tom to make it.

"No, wait. Please don't shoot, lady." Bolt quickly raised one hand in the air and shook it back and forth.

A chill went down his spine when the woman suddenly lunged toward him, her vacant eyes staring into his. The pistol was no more than five feet from his head and it was aimed right between his eyes.

"You can't stop me," she said in the oddly husked voice that was now calm and even. And sinister.

"No, please, woman. I haven't done anything to hurt you." Bolt raised his hand higher, waved it more frantically as he glimpsed Tom and saw that he was making headway as he crawled like a snake along the ground.

The shawled lady tossed her head back and laughed like a crazy old woman. Bolt started to make a move when she lunged at him again. He rolled his head to the side, made a grab for her arm. She jumped back, out of his reach.

"Where's my brother? Where is he, you low-down miserable swine?" the woman screamed hysterically as she took aim at Bolt's head. "Where is Randy?"

The husk was gone from her voice and her hand was shaking again.

"I don't know Randy," Bolt said.

"Yes you do. I know you do," she said in a trembling, high-pitched voice. "What have you done with my brother?"

"Nothing," Bolt said quickly.

"You killed him! You killed him!"

The woman leaned forward and tightened her finger around the trigger.

Bolt rolled away from her and cringed as he listened for the shot. He heard the sudden movement and opened his eyes.

Tom jumped up behind the crazed woman, his face and clothes covered with mud. He reached around and slammed the edge of his open hand against the woman's wrist.

The woman cried out in pain and released her grip on the cheap pistol. The gun made a dull thud when it hit the damp ground.

Both Bolt and the crazy woman grabbed for the loose gun. As Tom grabbed her from behind, the woman kicked the gun out of Bolt's reach. She broke free of Tom's clutches and whirled around, slapped him across the face.

Tom reached for her again and she dug her fingernails into the flesh of his arm, pulled at his tousled hair with the other hand.

Bolt jumped to his feet, ready to help subdue the crazy woman. Except for a spot on his chin, there was no dirt on his face, but his clothes and boots were filthy with mud.

Tom knocked the woman's hands away, grabbed her shoulders again and overpowered her. As she kicked and screamed and tried to bite his clutching fingers, he wrestled her to the ground in a flurry of petticoats as her skirt flew up around her waist.

Bolt was surprised when he saw the woman's long, slender legs, her trim ankles. These were not the legs of an old woman, he thought. He looked again at the strands of hair that stuck out from the woman's scarf. Gray? Light brown? He couldn't be sure in the fading light of dusk.

"Let me go! Let me go!" the woman screamed as Tom picked her up and set her on her feet.

"Not a chance," Tom said.

Bolt walked over and retrieved her pistol, stuck it in the top of his trousers. He picked up his dirty Stetson and stuck it on his head.

"Let me go, you swine," she screamed as she struggled with Tom.

"Calm down, miss," Bolt said. "You want to tell us what this is all about?"

"You know what it's about," she yelled, as she

132

kicked back at Tom's shin. "You killed my brother and you're going to pay for it."

Tom tightened his grip on her shoulders.

"Ouch! Let me go," she yelled as she tried to get away from him.

"We don't even know your brother and we'll let you go when you calm down." Bolt said.

"You do, too," she said. "Miss Belle told me you did."

"That figures," Tom said.

"What's your name, miss?" Bolt asked.

"I don't have to tell you."

"No, you don't, but if you want Tom to let you go, you're going to tell us what this is all about."

"And you're going to tell us why in the hell you tried to kill us," Tom said.

"Let me go and I'll tell you," she said.

"Let her go," Bolt said.

Tom dropped his hands from the girl's shoulders and walked around in front of her.

The girl brushed her muddy skirt back in place and glared at Tom. "You're both filthy swine," she said. "If you didn't have my gun, you'd be sorry."

"But we do have your gun," Bolt said. "And, I don't much like strangers coming on my property and taking shots at me and my friend. Now, are you going to tell us what's going on or not?"

The woman eyed each of them carefully and for a minute Bolt thought she was going to make a run for it. But suddenly, her shoulders drooped and she stared down at the ground for a minute.

133

When she looked up again, Bolt saw the anger in her eyes, the hurt.

"That woman, Miss Jessie Belle, over at that other . . . uh . . . house of pleasure," the girl stammered without looking directly at either one of them. "She told me that you had done something real bad to my brother."

"Look, miss, Bolt said. "We don't know who you are or who your brother is, but we haven't done anything bad to anyone. We might be able to help you if you'll tell us what happened."

"My name is Clarissa Mayfield."

"I'm Jared Bolt and this is my friend, Tom Penrod."

She nodded politely. "My brother is Randy Mayfield. Randy disappeared Monday night and I've been frantic about him ever since."

"I can understand that," Bolt said. "Is your brother a cattle drover?"

"No. Randy is just getting started in the cattle raising business and I moved here two months ago to help him."

"It's getting dark out here, Clarissa," Bolt said. "If you want to walk up to the house with us, we'll see if we can help you find your brother."

Clarissa eyed each of them again. "All right," she said after a minute.

"Tom, run over to the bordello and tell Harmony we're back and find out how Abby is."

Tom scooped up his hat and dashed off. By the time Bolt and Clarissa walked up the hill and reached the house, Tom had caught up with them.

"That didn't take long," Bolt said as he opened the door to the dark house.

"No, they laughed at me," Tom said. "Why in the hell didn't you tell me my face was muddy?"

Bolt lit the lantern on the table just inside the back door and stepped aside so Clarissa and Tom could enter. "Oh, Tom, you're a sight," Bolt laughed.

"I wouldn't laugh. Look at your ugly puss."

Bolt wiped at his chin and looked down at his mud-stained clothes.

"Mercy, look at my dress," Clarissa said. "You've ruined it."

"It'll wash," Bolt said as he carried the lantern into the kitchen and set it down on the table. "Sit down, Clarissa."

Clarissa fluffed her skirt out around her as she eased into a hardbacked chair. She sat up straight, her back not touching the chair. Bolt sat down across from her.

"Abby's much better," Tom said. "She's been up and walking around today. And Harmony says supper will be ready in fifteen minutes and not to bother to come to the table with dirty hands or faces."

Bolt laughed, then turned to Clarissa. "Do you live in San Antonio?" he asked.

"Five miles north of there. My brother Randy bought a big ranch with some of his inheritance money after our parents died."

Clarissa pulled the dirty scarf from her head and put it in her lap. Her hair fell into shape and framed her pretty face. Her hair was light brown, Bolt noticed, not gray as he'd first thought. And in the lamplight, her pale blue eyes sparkled and took on a deeper color.

It was as if he were seeing Clarissa Mayfield for the very first time, and he was genuinely stunned by her beauty.

"So Randy just disappeared from your ranch Monday night?" he said.

"Not exactly," Clarissa said. "Randy left the ranch early Monday afternoon. He rode to town because he wanted to withdraw enough money from his savings at the bank so he could buy some more cattle. His friend, Joe Bob Willis, told Randy that there would be a lot of cattle coming into the stockyards in San Antonio this week and if Randy wanted to get his pick of the cattle, he'd better go in early in the week. When Randy left the house Monday, he told me he'd be back before dark, but he never came home."

"Do you know if he got the money out of the bank?" Bolt asked. He noticed that Clarissa's face looked soft in the lamplight, but she sat stiff in the chair.

"Yes. I checked at the bank yesterday and the teller told me Randy withdrew a thousand dollars from his savings."

"So both Randy and the money are missing," Tom said from the kitchen counter where he was scrubbing his hands and face at the basin.

"Yes," said Clarissa. She glanced over at Tom, then back at Bolt. "I was very worried about Randy when he didn't come home Monday night, but I tried to convince myself that his horse threw a shoe or broke a leg, or maybe that the bank was closed by the time he got to town and he had decided to stay in San Antonio until the next day."

"Did you go looking for him Tuesday?" Bolt asked. He saw the slight movement of her arms and knew that she was nervously wringing the scarf in her lap.

"No, I figured Randy would be home for sure Tuesday." Clarissa lowered her head, then looked across the table at Bolt. "Besides, he's a grown boy. He's two years older than I am, and quite able to take care of himself. I've only been at the ranch a week, and I didn't know if he had a lady friend in town that he might have stayed all night with. If he did plan to stay the night with a lady friend, he'd certainly never tell me about it. I was brought up to be a proper lady, and Randy knows that sort of thing would shock me."

"Seems it would be better to know about it than to worry yourself sick about him," Bolt said.

"I'm beginning to think so," Clarissa said, "but being from Boston, I'm just not accustomed to the ways of the West."

"That sort of thing goes on all over the world, ma'am, not just in the West," Tom said as he dried his face with a towel.

"Not in Boston society, Mister Penrod," Clarissa said proudly. "My parents were very wealthy, and even if they hadn't been, they knew how to conduct themselves properly and so did all of our friends."

"And society people always wait until they're married before they . . ."

"Say what you want, Mister Penrod," Clarissa snapped, "but I've never known a rude person until I came out West."

"How old is your brother?" Bolt asked. He didn't care about Randy's age. He was just curious about Clarissa.

"Randy's twenty-three," she said.

And that made her twenty-one, Bolt thought. "So Randy didn't come home again Tuesday night."

"No, and by the time I realized he wasn't coming home, it was too late and too dark for me to go looking for him. I was so worried, I was beside myself. I didn't sleep a wink Tuesday night and I started out first thing the next morning to find him. I went to the bank first, of course."

"Did you go out to the stockyards?" Bolt asked.

"Heavens, no. It wouldn't be proper for a lady to be around the stockyards with all those grubby men. I've heard about those cattle drovers."

"They aren't bad," said Bolt. "Hell, they're lonely and dusty from the trail, and ready for a few drinks and a night on the town after their long trek, but most of them are hard-working, decent men."

"Well, I didn't want to go out there, so I looked for Randy's friend, Joe Bob, although I didn't know anything about him. He's been out to the ranch a couple of times to visit Randy, but of course, being a lady, I left them alone and never listened to their conversations."

"Maybe you should have," Tom commented as he dragged a chair out and sat down.

"Did you find Joe Bob?" Bolt asked. He was annoyed by Clarissa's arrogant attitude, but equally fascinated by her elegance and by the way the lamplight danced in her pale eyes, sometimes turning them to gold when she turned just right.

"Not until this morning," she said. "And then it was quite by accident. I stayed at a hotel in town last night because I couldn't face staying at the ranch by myself another night. And when I went into the hotel dining room for breakfast this morning, Joe Bob was the one who came to take my order. He's the cook at the hotel, of all things."

"So what'd he say?" Bolt said.

Clarissa sat up even straighter in the chair. "I'm ashamed to admit it, but Joe Bob said that he and Randy went to The Proud Peacock Monday evening. I find it very difficult to believe that my brother would go to such a sinful place."

"There's nothing wrong with brothels, ma'am,"

Bolt said.

"I would expect you to say such a thing, being the owner of one yourself," Clarissa said with a haughty tilt to her head. "As far as I'm concerned, all brothels should be shut down forever. I have no respect for the people who run them, and even less respect for the hussies who work in them."

"Present company included?" Bolt said.

"Yes."

"You've got your head buried in the sand, lady," Tom said.

"So be it," said Clarissa. "I wouldn't be here if I weren't desperate about Randy."

"We'll help you find him if we can," Bolt said. "Maybe you'll change your mind about us."

"I doubt it," Clarissa said sarcastically. "People like you tempt innocent men like my brother into a sinful way of life. And now Randy's gone. I'll tell you what I know and then I'll leave."

"I'm listening," Bolt said.

"Joe Bob said he and Randy had a couple of drinks while they waited for . . . for a soiled dove. Joe Bob said he had his turn first and when he came downstairs after being with the soiled dove, Randy was still waiting his turn. Joe Bob told Randy he had to get back to town because he had to get up early to cook breakfast at the hotel the next morning. Joe Bob didn't know Randy was missing until I told him this morning."

Bolt thought about what Pete Pensor, the clerk

at the stockyards, had told him about the three drovers who didn't come back for their gear after visiting The Proud Peacock. And Abby had mentioned that one of her customers hadn't come back to see her as promised. And now Clarissa's brother was missing.

He realized that Jessie Belle was involved in something more terrible than just running a whorehouse that catered to rough men. The Proud Peacock was just a front for something far more devious. He was sure of it. But what?

Bolt felt the hackles rise on the back of his neck.

# CHAPTER TWELVE

"Seems to me your brother disappeared mysteriously from The Proud Peacock," Bolt said.

"Oh, no," Clarissa said. She shook her head emphatically. "I rode to The Proud Peacock this afternoon and talked to Jessie Belle myself. I didn't go inside the brothel, you understand, but she came outside and talked to me. She said she remembered my brother, and that Randy got tired of waiting for a girl, and that he came over here to the Rocking Bar."

"Bullshit," said Tom.

Clarissa winced. "I beg your pardon," she said.

"What's the matter, lady?" Tom sneered. "You never heard that word before?"

"As a matter of fact, I haven't," Clarissa said as she looked down her nose at Tom. "Where I come from, gentlemen don't speak that way in front of a lady. You two are the crudest men I've ever met."

"Your brother never came here, Clarissa," Bolt said. "We've only had one customer all week, and that was Clem Atkins, an old cowhand."

"Miss Belle says different and I believe her," Clarissa insisted.

"Well, Jessie Belle's full of shit," Tom said. "Your brother sure as hell didn't come over here."

"Watch your filthy tongue," Clarissa said.

Tom's chair legs scraped across the floor as he shoved the chair back and stood up. "Don't tell me what to do, you ungrateful bitch," he shouted. "This is our house, not yours."

"Well, I never," Clarissa said as she stood up in a huff. She stuffed her dirty scarf in a skirt pocket.

"I can believe that, and you probably never will," Tom laughed. "No man in his right mind would have you. You'd cut his balls off."

"Oh, you . . . you . . . you filthy-minded swine," she shouted.

"I'll bet you'd love to call me a dirty bastard," Tom laughed.

"Yes, I certainly would."

Tom turned to Bolt. "I'm going down to the bordello for supper," he said. "I'll see you down there if you can tear yourself away from Miss Priss." A minute later, he went out the back door and slammed it shut behind him.

"You go join your friends," Clarissa said as she brushed nervously at her skirt. "I have to be going now."

Bolt stood up. He knew that Tom had purposely tried to irritate Clarissa because of her haughty attitude toward bordellos. Bolt didn't mind. In fact, he rather enjoyed it. After all,

Clarissa had come here to kill them, just like Jessie Belle had done. And Clarissa had damned near succeeded.

But Bolt saw a big difference between the two girls. While Jessie Belle was hard and brittle, Bolt sensed a softness beneath Clarissa's tough exterior. Jessie acted out of greed and her involvement with unscrupulous characters. Clarissa acted out of desperation for her brother. Jessie was arrogant and had nothing to back it up. No grace, no kindness, no warmth, no feeling for anyone else. Clarissa was arrogant, too, but she was also refined and poised, and gentle. She had been raised to be prim and proper, and her apparent arrogance was a part of that structured upbringing.

Bolt smiled when he thought of Clarissa helping Randy with the cattle. She would get her hands dirty and stand ankle deep in cow shit. Living on her brother's ranch would take some of the starch out of her society bonnet.

"Tom gets that way when he's hungry," Bolt said as a half-hearted apology.

"I was stunned to hear such foul language, but I can't really blame him," Clarissa said. "I've been a most unwelcome intruder."

"Well, you did have your moments out there by the stable. How'd you get here? I didn't notice a stray horse."

"I rode," Clarissa said. "I hid my horse behind the stable. Oh, I must have been crazy to come out here after you and Tom. I can't believe I actually tried to kill you."

"Fear can do strange things to people, and you're afraid for your brother."

"But I don't even know how to use a gun."

"You'd better learn before you go after anyone else. You're downright dangerous the way you are. Will you stay and have supper with us?"

"No thank you, Mister Bolt. I'm not hungry enough to eat in a brothel."

Bolt shrugged his shoulders. "Suit yourself," he said. "And drop the Mister. It's just Bolt, to friend and foe alike." He left the lantern burning in the kitchen and walked toward the back door. He took another lamp from a shelf in the small entrance room and touched a match to the wick. When the lamp flickered to a full glow, he carried it outside where it was fully dark. He waited until Clarissa came outside, then closed the door.

He saw her eyes widen as she looked out into the broad expanse of darkness, as if she were searching for the croaking frogs. He thought he saw her shudder as she glanced up at the sky where there was no moon and the stars were hidden by clouds. She pulled her shawl up around her neck, even though it was still warm outside.

"Bolt, will you help me find Randy?" she asked, her voice soft, as if she were suddenly timid.

"Yes. I'll do everything I can." He held the lantern high in the air to light their path as they made their way down the porch steps and across the small stretch of damp grass to the set of steps that led down the hill.

Below, two flickering lanterns hung at the front entrance of the bordello, one on each side of the door. Lamplight spilled from most of the windows and splashed across the grass. Off to the left, way beyond the dark stable, the bunkhouse windows glowed with their own light.

Clarissa clutched the handrail as she went down the steep steps, feeling out each wooden plank with her high-top shoes before she put her full weight on it.

Holding the lantern in front of them, Bolt walked right beside her on the narrow steps, shifting his weight when she did, brushing up against her arm more than once. For the first time, he smelled her delicate scent and the night breeze seemed suddenly hot.

A coyote howled in the distance and briefly blotted out the sound of the singing frogs. Clarissa gasped and grabbed his arm.

"It's just a coyote," he said.

She quickly moved her hand away from his arm. "I know. Being a city girl, I'm just not used to the wild animals yet."

"Things sound spookier at night, but that coyote is a long way off." Bolt knew she shuddered, even though he couldn't see it.

When they got to the bottom of the steps, Clarissa paused and glanced toward the bunkhouse.

"Is that the stable over there, all lit up?" she asked.

"No, the stable is all dark," he said. "That

building with the lamplight is the bunkhouse where the cowhands live."

"Oh," she said.

Bolt detected the disappointment in her voice and knew she was frightened of the dark.

"Clarissa, I think you should stay here tonight. I don't like to think of you riding back to town all by yourself."

"I'm a big girl, Bolt," she said, a slight quiver to her voice.

"I know you are, but it's dark out there and it's a long way to town. One of our girls is working at The Proud Peacock now, so there's an extra bedroom in the bordello. You're welcome to use it."

"How dare you suggest such a thing," Clarissa said.

"What? I offered you a place to sleep."

"I won't sleep in a whorehouse."

"It's not like you think," Bolt said. "The cribs are out back, behind the bordello."

"What cribs?" she asked and Bolt knew she didn't have any idea what he was talking about.

"The cribs are the separate cottages out back. That's where the harlots take the men. The customers wait in the living room of the bordello, but they don't sleep with the harlots in there."

"Oh."

"You would be sleeping in the living quarters of the bordello, in one of the upstairs bedrooms, where no men are allowed. You'll have your privacy because each girl has her own room. And Harmony, the madam . . . the house mother, she sleeps downstairs."

Clarissa thought about it for a minute.

"No, I just couldn't sleep in there."

"Well, it's all we've got to offer unless you want to sleep in my bed or Tom's."

She tilted her head up and Bolt could see the reflection of lamplight in her wide, questioning eyes.

"That sounds like an indecent proposition to me," she said in an accusing tone.

"Take it any way you want to, Clarissa, but I'm not giving up my bed when there's a nice clean one waiting for you in the bordello."

"But the . . . the harlots will be in there."

Bolt's temper flared. "Yes, they'll be there. That's where they live. Are you afraid you'll be contaminated by them?"

"No, not really," she said meekly, "but I've heard about harlots."

"They're nice, decent girls, just like you."

Clarissa glanced toward the dark stable, then over at the brightly-lit bordello.

"No, I just can't bring myself to sleep in a whorehouse," she said.

"Ride on back to town then," Bolt said as he pulled her pistol from his waistband and handed it to her. "Here's your pistol. You might need it. No telling what kind of man or beast you'll run into on the dark, desolate, lonely road between here and San Antonio. But I'm sure it couldn't be as scary as sleeping in the same house with five harlots and a madam."

He turned and walked away, leaving Clarissa speechless, and in the dark. He carried the lantern high, listening for her footsteps on the damp grass behind him as he strolled toward the bordello. He heard nothing but the constant hum of the frogs down by the stream.

Just before he reached the steps to the bordello porch, the frogs suddenly stopped croaking. The night became deathly still, and Bolt sensed trouble.

An owl hooted a warning from a high tree somewhere near the bunkhouse.

Bolt heard Clarissa squeal. "Just an owl," he called back over his shoulder.

And then the silence was broken by the loud, eerie howl of a nearby coyote. A second howl followed on top of the first one as a closer coyote answered the call. Bolt was accustomed to the sounds. He knew the coyotes were down by the stream.

"Oh! Oh dear," cried Clarissa.

Bolt turned around and saw her running toward him, tripping over her own feet as she ran. He held the lantern high and walked back to help her. She dashed up and threw her arms around him. He put one arm around her shoulder and felt her tremble.

"Did you change your mind about staying the night?" he asked.

"Yes. Oh, yes. I'll sleep anywhere tonight, just so I don't have to ride back to town all by myself."

Bolt escorted her up the steps and dropped his

arm when they were on the porch where it was bright. He hung the lantern on an empty hook.

"Come on in and eat with us," Bolt said.

Clarissa glanced down at her blue, flared skirt and brushed at the mud stains, which were clearly visible in the lamplight.

"I can't go in there looking like this," she said. "What would the harlots think?"

"They won't judge you by your clothes."

"Goodness, I hope not."

"Don't worry about it. It's my guess that they'll take to you easier than you take to them."

"Why would you say that?"

"Because you already have a notion fixed in your head about what prostitutes are like. You've tagged them with a label. They don't have you tagged, so they'll accept you just as you are."

"But they don't know me." Clarissa said.

"You don't know them either."

"No, but I know what they do. Everyone knows that prostitutes are shameless hussies who have no respect for their own bodies."

"See what I mean, Clarissa? You've put a label on them when you don't even know them. They're decent women, just like you."

"You're not only insulting, Bolt, you're argumentative as well."

"I've been called worse."

"With good reason, I'm sure." She brushed at her skirt again. "I brought extra clothes with me because I didn't know how long I'd be staying in town when I left my ranch. I really should get my

150

carpeting and change my dress."

"Why? So you can prove to everyone that you're better than the whores? That's bullshit."

"You're very crude, Bolt."

"I'm also a very decent chap once you get to know me."

"I'm sure I won't have that pleasure," Clarissa said sarcastically. "My carpetbag should be brought in. It's tied to my horse's saddle."

"Don't look at me," Bolt said. "I ain't gonna walk out there in the dark."

"But I need it. It's got my nightgown in it."

"Then maybe you'll just have to sleep in the buff tonight."

"You have a naughty tongue, Mister Bolt."

"And you have a naughty mind. Come on, I'll buy you supper."

The smell of freshly-baked biscuits assaulted his nostrils and made his mouth water as he opened the door and waited for Clarissa to enter.

When she looked up at him, the lamplight bathed her face in a soft glow and he was taken with her natural beauty. He squinted slightly and tried to picture her as a Boston socialite, with fancy clothes, makeup and expensive jewelry, and hair that was arranged just so. He decided he liked her just the way she was, mud and all.

"Bolt, what's it like to be a whore?" she asked as she stepped inside.

"I wouldn't know," he laughed. "You'll have to ask the girls."

Clarissa gazed around the large living room as

they walked through it.

"It's so clean in here," she said.

"What'd you expect?"

"I don't know. I thought it would be dingy and smelly."

"Harmony and the girls take pride in this place. They keep it clean."

"You mean the harlots clean the house?"

"Yes, they do a lot of things around here besides spreading their legs."

Clarissa shuddered. "Don't say things like that."

"Well, it's true. The girls do all the cooking and the mending, and the laundry. They work in the garden. They even make their own clothes."

"I'll bet it doesn't take much fabric for their clothes."

"What do you mean?"

"They wear very skimpy outfits that scarcely cover their bodies, from what I've been told."

"Yes, they wear sensual clothing," he said as he led her into the kitchen.

Harmony was alone in the kitchen and she stood near the woodstove, a big lid in her hand. She wore a light blue frock with a high collar and a long skirt. She wore no jewelry and only a touch of rouge on her cheeks. Her long blond hair was pulled back away from her face and tied in place with a blue ribbon.

"I brought company for supper," Bolt said.

"Good," Harmony smiled. "I'll put an extra plate on. I hope you like beef stew and biscuits."

"Yes, I do," said Clarissa.

"Harmony, this is Clarissa Mayfield," Bolt said. "She's just recently moved here from Boston."

"Nice to know you, Clarissa," Harmony said as she set the lid down. She smiled at Clarissa, then began dishing the stew into a large porcelain bowl.

"Clarissa, this is Harmony Sanchez. She's the madam here at the bordello, and, as you can see, chief cook."

Clarissa's eyes widened with surprise. "I'm pleased to meet you."

"Clarissa is going to spend the night and I told her she could sleep down here with you girls," Bolt said.

"Good," said Harmony. "She can sleep in Doris' room. Supper's ready, so you two had better go in and sit down. The others are already in the dining room."

"I hear Abby's feeling better," Bolt said.

"Yes. She came downstairs for supper tonight."

"I'm glad," Bolt said. "Do you need some help?"

"No, the girls will help me carry the food in. Just take Clarissa in and introduce her to everybody."

Bolt watched Clarissa's face when he took her into the dining room. He could tell she was nervous as everyone turned to look at her.

"We have a guest for supper tonight," he announced as he glanced around. He was glad to see that the table was set with the good china and crystal goblets, and that all of the girls wore

153

simple, modest dresses. Even Cathy Boring wore a plain frock instead of the harlot costume she'd been wearing in hopes that they would get some customers.

Clarissa glanced first at the three girls who stood nearby, then at the two who sat at the table with Tom. Her expression changed to a slight frown when she noticed Abby's black eye. She lowered her head when she met Tom's gaze.

"This is Clarissa Mayfield and she's going to be spending the night with you girls," Bolt said, and then went on to introduce her all the way around. "And you already know Tom."

"Yes," Clarissa said.

"Clarissa is a Boston socialite," Bolt said.

The other girls looked at her with excited faces.

"I'm afraid I don't look much like a socialite tonight," Clarissa said with embarrassment as she glanced down at her muddy dress.

"That's all right," Linda laughed. "We don't look much like prostitutes tonight, either."

"No, you don't," Clarissa smiled timidly. "At least not like I'd pictured you."

"Come sit by me," Abby said as she patted the seat next to her. "I want to hear all about what it's like to be a socialite."

"Only if you tell me what it's like to be a harlot," Clarissa said.

"We'll save that until after supper, when the men have gone back up to their house," Winny Hart said with a twinkle in her eye.

"Damn, I guess I'll never find out," Bolt said.

"And to answer your question, Clarissa, Abby got her black eye while she was working over at The Proud Peacock, not here."

"I didn't ask a question," Clarissa said.

"No, but you thought it. Harmony won't allow these girls to be hurt. She'll kick the customers out on their butts if they even think about roughing up one of the girls."

"I do have a question, though," Clarissa said as she sat down between Abby and Winny Hart. "What's Bolt really like?"

"We'll save that for later, too," Winny grinned. "We wouldn't want to embarrass him."

# CHAPTER THIRTEEN

Bolt woke up early to the smell of coffee and bacon. He washed his face with water from the basin, then dressed before he went into the kitchen.

Harmony yawned as he walked in.

"Good morning, sleepyhead," Bolt said.

"Oh, these late nights get to me. We girls sat in the living room and talked until after midnight. I finally sent the girls upstairs and went to bed. But I heard them laughing and chattering for at least another hour."

"I take it Clarissa got along with the girls."

"Of course. She was the hit of the party. The girls loved her."

Harmony dished up their plates and the two of them ate by themselves.

"You know, she didn't really want to stay in the bordello last night," Bolt said as he buttered a hot biscuit and took a bite. "She thought harlots were filthy sluts and she didn't want to be associated with them."

"I know. She told us," Harmony laughed. "But I think we changed her mind. In fact, when we found out Clarissa didn't have a nightgown with

156

her, we all offered her one of ours and she picked one of Cathy's gowns, the sexiest black night-gown in the bunch."

"I'll be damned."

"And the girls told her all about you," Harmony said with a teasing smile.

"They better not have."

"I'll be surprised if she's still speaking to you today."

Bolt stood up and stretched when he was through eating. "When Tom gets up, tell him I've gone into town. I'll be back before noon."

Bolt arrived at the stockyards shortly after nine o'clock. He rode around the area, but didn't see Lyle Watley. Finally, he reined his horse up at the hitchrail in front of the office. After he tied Nick up, he sat on one of the long hard benches in front of the office where he could see anyone who came near the stockyards.

He didn't have to wait long. An older fellow joined Bolt on the bench and struck up a conver-sation. A few minutes after that, Bolt saw Watley ride up to another hitchrail that was just outside the fenced-in pens. Watley tied his horse to the hitchrail, then started to walk toward the office.

When Watley saw Bolt sitting on the bench, he stopped abruptly, hesitated, glared at Bolt, then turned and walked the other way.

"That's that young feller from The Proud Pea-cock, ain't it?" said the grizzled old man named Roger. He pulled a thin-bladed pocket knife and a chunk of wood the size of a stubby broomstick out of his pocket and set to whittling.

"Yeah. Lyle Watley." Bolt said.

"Ey what?" said the old man as he leaned closer to Bolt and turned his good ear that way. "I cain't hear too good because of those danged bawling cattle. Speak up, sonny."

"I said that's Lyle Watley. Do you know him?" Bolt asked as he ducked a chip of wood that flew out from the man's whittling.

"Not really, although he's spoke to me before. He's tried to get me to come on out to that whorehouse where he works a couple of times, but hell, I'm too danged old for that sort of foolishness."

"You're never too old," Bolt said as he watched Watley walk up to young man who stood near the entrance to the corral. The man Watley spoke to wore dark brown trousers that looked clean and crisp, a leather vest over a long-sleeved shirt, and a red bandanna tied around his neck. He pushed his hat back on his head when Watley spoke to him. A dark brown Stetson, Bolt thought, but he couldn't be sure from that distance. The man was obviously not a newly-arrived drover. His clothes weren't rumpled enough.

"Ey what?" the old man said. "Speak into my good ear, sonny."

"I said you're never too old for a pretty woman. Do you come out to the stockyards very often?"

"I'm here most every mornin', unless it be rainin'," said Roger. "It passes the time of day for me and I always enjoy sittin' around and jawin' with fellows like yourself."

"How often does Watley come out here?"

"Well," said Roger as he sliced a narrow sliver of wood from the chunk, "that young feller Watley seems to be the first one on the scene when a trailherd is comin' through, and then he just sort of disappears for a spell."

"Is that right?" Bolt said, his head turned slightly so he could keep his eye on Watley and the fellow with him.

"Yair. And from what I hear tell, they's been a few drovers disappear about the same time." Roger leaned around Bolt and peered out at Watley.

"Oh?"

"Yair. Like them three drovers old Pete was tellin' me about. I saw 'em talkin' to Watley before they left and they still ain't come after the gear they stored here last Monday. And here it is Friday already. It just don't figure."

"Yeah, Pete told me about that." Bolt saw both Watley and the neat-looking man glance his way at the same time as they were talking.

"There've been rumors that some other drovers has just suddenly dropped out of sight," the old man said, "but I cain't say as they'd talked to Watley. I learn a lot just sittin' here all mornin' listenin' to other folks talk."

"I'll bet you do," Bolt said. He watched the man Watley had been talking to nod his head, then mount a black stallion and ride away. The fellow glanced over at Bolt as he passed by.

Bolt listened to the old man chatter on, but he

kept his attention focused on Lyle Watley. A minute later he saw Watley stroll across the manure-littered yards to greet a couple of scraggly-looking drovers who were still bringing in their herd of cattle.

Bolt chatted with the old man for a few minutes more, then excused himself.

"I'd stay away from that Watley feller, if I was you," Roger said.

"I plan to."

Bolt rode away, wondering what the two men had been talking about. He had a feeling it concerned him. He kept a careful watch on his back trail, and on the road ahead as he rode toward the ranch. He was almost home when he started thinking about Clarissa and her missing brother, Randy Mayfield.

The ambusher burst through the tall bushes at the side of the road and appeared suddenly on the trail just ahead of Bolt, pistol drawn and cocked. The man jerked the reins up hard and brought his horse to a dirt-spraying halt, blocking Bolt's path. He thrust his gun hand forward and squeezed the trigger.

Bolt saw the flash of the red bandanna at the man's throat, the leather vest, the dark brown Stetson, just before he threw himself to the side and out of the saddle. His white Stetson, still carrying the mud stains from the night before, tumbled from his head, hit the dirt, and rolled across the road.

The shot rang out before Bolt hit the ground, his boot still laced in the stirrup. He jerked his foot free and rolled away from his horse just as the ambusher rode around the animal and took aim again.

Bolt rolled toward the thick bushes, unable to snake his pistol free from its holster before the horseman fired again.

The bullet whizzed over Bolt's head, missing him by inches. As the ambusher and horse skirted around Bolt's horse and loomed down on him, Bolt crawled into the bushes and got to his knees, jerked his pistol out and tripped the hammer back.

He stayed perfectly still and heard the metal click of the henchman's pistol being cocked. He waited for the shot to ring out, not daring to move as much as blinking his eyelids. Instead, he heard the slow shuffle of the horse's hooves as the killer moved his horse around.

Bolt saw the shadow then. At the base of the dense bushes, where the foliage was not so thick. He studied the slowly-moving shadow that fell across the small space of bare dirt between two closely bunched bushes. The space of bare dirt was not more than eight inches long and four inches wide, but it was all Bolt needed to make out the shadowy shape of a horse's spindly leg.

Bolt raised his head slowly and saw a small sliver of the brim of the man's dark hat as it appeared at the top of the tall bushes in front of Bolt. The two enemies were not more than five feet away from each other with only the thick shrubbery between them.

The sliver of hat moved to the right and out of

Bolt's sight and when he glanced down, he saw that the hoof shadow was gone. He heard the creaking of the man's saddle as the horseman walked his horse a few feet along the row of brush.

Bolt let the breath out that he had been holding in. An instant later, the hoof shadow appeared again on the bare piece of dirt and Bolt knew the henchman wouldn't stray far from that spot. Not far enough for Bolt to get the jump on the man.

He glanced around for something heavy and spotted a small rock just out of reach. He knew if he could throw the rock some distance away, he could distract the ambusher long enough to get the advantage. He looked up and saw the sliver of hat brim above the line of green leaves. And then he caught a glint of the man's wavering pistol through the thick foliage.

Bolt had two choices. He could judge the rider's position by the sliver of hat brim, and aim for the heart. But if he missed, even by an inch, it would be all over for him. The rider would press his advantage and fire before Bolt could get a second shot off.

He chose his other alternative, although it was just as risky. Still on his knees, and with his pistol still aimed in the man's direction, Bolt leaned over slowly and reached for the rock. As he shifted his weight, a twig snapped under his leg.

Bolt froze and heard the creak of leather as the man turned in his saddle. Without hesitation, Bolt glanced up at the moving hat brim, brought his sights down two feet and squeezed the trigger, blind to his target. As he shot he threw himself forward and hugged the ground, face down.

Bolt's shots cracked the air within a split second of each other. His muscles tautened as he cringed, expecting a bullet to tear into some part of his body. It was only a fraction of a second, but it seemed like an eternity before he heard a bullet thud into flesh. He waited for the pain.

He heard the man grunt, and the beginning of a groan. An instant later, he heard the *whoosh thunk* of the second bullet smashing into the ground, an inch away from Bolt's left boot. If he had still been in a kneeling position the ambusher's bullet would have zeroed in on its target.

The ambusher's moan was cut off short and followed by a giant thud as the man rolled off his horse and crashed to the ground.

Prone on the ground, Bolt moved only enough to bring his pistol around and ease the hammer back with his thumb. And then he waited, again without moving a muscle.

The air was soundless, except for the loud thump of his heart beating in his chest. And then one of the horses whinnied and Bolt felt the shock of adrenaline dump into his system.

He waited, motionless, for several more minutes, until his heartbeat slowed, and heard only the scuffling of the horses' hooves as they milled around.

Finally, Bolt lowered his head to the ground and peered out through the base of the bushes.

He moved just enough to see a portion of the man's body, and what he saw sickened him. He saw only the man's chest, the hole where the blood spilled out and stained the white shirt, the leather vest lying open.

Bolt pushed himself up on his knees, pulled the bushes aside and crawled through to the blood-spattered road. When he saw the ambusher's vacant stare, the gaping mouth, the leg that hung lifeless from the stirrup where the man's boot was caught, Bolt slid his pistol back in his holster and shook his head.

He stood there for a minute, stunned by the sight of the dead man, suddenly frightened by how close he'd come to his own death. And then he walked over and untangled the man's boot from the stirrup and let the leg fall to the ground.

Nick came up and nudged Bolt with his cold, wet nose. Bolt patted the horse and breathed a deep sigh.

It took Bolt some fifteen minutes and a great deal of effort to lift the dead weight of the man's body and juggle it up and over across the saddle of the black stallion. He tugged and pulled some more until the dead man was face down over the saddle, his head and arms falling over one side of the horse, his legs hanging down from the other side.

He reached into his own saddlebags and dug out enough twine to tie the already-stiffening body in place atop the black horse. He picked up the ambusher's dark hat, stuffed it under the tight twine, then walked over and retrieved his own Stetson and slipped it on his head.

He headed the stallion back toward town and slapped it hard across the rump.

"Take him home, boy," he said to the horse. "I want him to deliver a message."

He watched the stallion move at a slow gait for a long time, then turned away and mounted Nick.

Bolt knew that Lyle Watley was wise to the fact that Bolt was checking up on him. From now on, he'd have to watch over his shoulder.

The game had now become deadly.

# CHAPTER FOURTEEN

Harmony and Clarissa were in the kitchen of the big ranch house when Bolt got home. They sat at the table, snapping fresh beans from the garden.

Bolt had already washed the blood from his hands, using the bucket of water he kept outside the stable. He wore clean, wrinkled clothes now, having stripped out of the blood-stained pants and shirt in the stable and putting on the extra set of clothes he always carried in his saddlebags.

He knew that Harmony noticed his change of clothes as soon as he walked in the door, and he was glad she didn't question him about it in front of Clarissa. The girl was so worried about her brother, he didn't want her to know how bad things were.

He saw that Clarissa wore a clean, light blue frock that seemed to give her pale blue eyes more color. It was a dress she'd brought from Boston, he figured, judging from the small pearl buttons down the front of the dress and the fine lace that adorned the bib and high collar of the gown. He saw that her hair was no longer straggly, but hung in soft, clean curls about her face.

"I'll fix you some lunch," Harmony said as she dropped the unsnapped beans in her hand back in the big tin pail that sat between the two girls. "The rest of us have already eaten."

"I'm not hungry," Bolt said, "but I'll take a cup of coffee if you have it."

"I'll get it," Clarissa said as she jumped up from the table. "Sit down, Bolt."

Bolt sat down across the table from where Clarissa had been sitting and watched the back of her lovely long dress float behind her as she walked gracefully across the floor. She took a cup and saucer from the cupboard, then turned to face him.

"Do you want sugar and cream in your coffee?" she asked.

"No thanks. Just black."

Bolt noticed Clarissa's figure for the first time and was impressed by the way she carried herself. Her back was straight, her shoulders thrown back so that her firm breasts formed nicely rounded mounds beneath the bodice of her gown. Her small waistline accented the curves of her breast, her slender neck. He studied her profile as she walked over to the stove and realized that he hadn't seen her figure before. She had hidden it behind that dark blue shawl she'd worn the night before.

She set the cup of steaming coffee in front of him and went back to snapping beans.

"Did you find out anything about my brother while you were in town?" she asked.

Bolt saw the hopeful look of expectation in her eyes as she looked at him from across the table.

"No, not yet," he said and saw her expression change to one of sad desperation. "Evidently your brother isn't the only one who's disappeared under mysterious circumstances. At least three cattle drovers disappeared the same day as Randy did."

"Are you sure?" Harmony asked.

"Yes. I did some checking at the stockyards and it seems the drovers went to The Proud Peacock, same as Randy did. I'll find him, Clarissa, so please don't worry about it."

"I know you'll try," she said. "I want to apologize for the way I acted last night."

"None needed. I was rather rude myself, as you pointed out several times."

"Harmony and the girls told me a lot about you last night," Clarissa said.

"All good, I hope," Bolt said with a cocky grin.

"I sure as heck didn't say anything nice about you," Harmony said with a straight face.

"Yes, you did, Harmony," Clarissa smiled. "All of the girls had good things to say about you, Bolt. I was wrong about you and Tom. I realize now that you really are involved in cattle ranching and that the brothel is merely a sideline."

"And a darned good money maker, if I do say so myself," Harmony said without looking up.

"Harmony's right," Bolt said. "She gets all the credit for making the brothel work."

"And all the blame when it doesn't work," Harmony added.

"That's not what you were saying last night, Harmony," Clarissa said.

"No, but I don't want Bolt's head to swell up any bigger than it already is." She smirked at Bolt as she stood up. "Now, if you two will excuse me."

"Where're you going, Harmony?" Bolt asked.

"Down to the bordello where I don't have to listen to a bunch of bull," she smiled. "Actually, Linda wanted to talk to you and I'll go down and let her know you're home."

"Is there a problem?" Bolt asked.

"Not that I know of," Harmony said.

"I was wrong about Harmony and the girls, too," Clarissa said after Harmony was gone. "They weren't anything like what I expected."

"I told you that you had them tagged wrong," Bolt said.

"I know. I can't believe that a whore or a madam could be so decent and wholesome, so caring."

"The ones who work for me are a special breed," Bolt said as he reached for a bean and snapped it in half. He tossed it in the big crock where the snapped beans were being placed. "Not all whores are good and decent, no more than all society women are good and decent. You'll find real bitches in both classes. That's why I hated to see you pre-judge them by their label."

"I've got to admit, I might have felt differently about them if they had looked like whores, but they're just ordinary people. They were so good to me I felt like a sister to them. In fact, your harlots have more of a family life here than I ever had growing up at home with those prissy, high society friends of my parents around all the time."

"I'm glad you like them, Clarissa."

"I know Harmony does a lot for the girls, but so do you and Tom. You don't look down on them because of what they do, and that's important to them. They told me that you've given them a good home where they're free to do what they want to. They said you never cheat them or insist that they do the things Jessie Belle makes her girls do. And they said that if they ever marry, they know their secrets are safe with you and Bolt. I have a lot of respect for you, Bolt."

"And did they tell you what it's like to be a whore?"

"That's none of your damned business, Bolt," Clarissa said with a snicker.

Bolt heard the back door open and hoped it was Tom. He needed to talk to him.

Linda Ramsey came through the doorway, her long blond curls bouncing across her shoulders. "I ran into Harmony on the path. She said you were back."

"You got a problem?"

"Nope. No problem," Linda said cheerfully. "By the way, Clarissa, Harmony told me to ask you to bring the beans down when you're through with them so she can set them to cooking."

"I just finished," Clarissa said. "I'll take them down and come back later to clean up the mess." She picked up the large crock and carried it out the back door.

"Bolt, I've decided to go over to The Proud Peacock and see if I can get Jessie Belle to hire me on," Linda announced.

Bolt scooted his chair back and stood up, his face suddenly flushed.

"What in the hell are you saying?" he roared. "You're not going over there."

"Yes I am, Bolt."

"I won't let you go. Not after what happened to Abby."

"You can't stop me, Bolt, but calm down. It's not what you think it is. I want to go over to The Proud Peacock just long enough to get Doris out of there before anything tragic happens to her."

"She made her choice," Bolt said. "And you heard Abby say that she couldn't talk Doris into leaving when she did. What makes you think you can persuade her to come back?"

"Because I can be very persuasive when I want to be. Besides, I have other reasons for going."

"Like what?"

"I feel sorry for Clarissa, Bolt, and I want to go over there to see if I can find out what happened to her brother. The only way I can get in over there is to become a whore for them."

"Absolutely not," Bolt said firmly. "I'm not going to risk having you hurt like Abby was."

"I'll be careful, Bolt."

"You have no defense against brutal men like the one who attacked Abby. And Jessie Belle sure as hell isn't going to keep them out of her whorehouse when she can make a lot of money off them."

"I don't care about that," Linda said. "I don't know what's going on over there at The Proud Peacock, but whatever it is, it isn't normal. Randy Mayfield could be dead by now. Or kidnapped, at the least. And I don't imagine Randy's the only one who's run into foul play over there."

"He isn't," Bolt said.

Linda tilted her head. "What do you mean?"

Bolt wished he hadn't mentioned it. "I found out that a few other men have disappeared after visiting The Proud Peacock."

"Then that's all the more reason I should go over there and spy on them. Somebody's got to put an end to whatever corruption they're involved in."

"Well, it's not going to be you, Linda. It's a man's job."

"Posh. I'm the logical one to go. Please, Bolt. I promise I'll just stay until I can get Doris out of there."

"No, Linda. You are not going over to The Proud Peacock. End of conversation."

"My mind's made up, Bolt."

"So's mine."

"Won't you listen to me, Bolt? I'm the only one who could get away with worming my way into their good graces and then spying on them. They'd never suspect me if I handled it right."

172

"Don't be too sure about that," Bolt yelled. "Jessie Belle is cunning enough to figure out what you were doing over there."

Linda smiled, a teasing look in her eyes.

"Maybe you'd be surprised to find out how cunning I can be."

"Maybe I would," Bolt said. "But you're still not going, Linda. I just won't let you do it. I refuse to let you risk your life so we can find out what they're up to."

Linda sighed and let her shoulders droop. "Well, Bolt, we've reached a stalemate."

"Yes we have, Linda," he said in a calmer tone. "I'm glad you finally agree with me."

"I don't," said Linda. "My bags are already packed and Tom has one of the horses waiting for me out front. I'm going to ride over to The Proud Peacock right now and apply for a job as a whore. I won't be back until I've accomplished what I want to do."

Linda turned on her heel and ran toward the front door.

"Linda, wait!" he shouted as he dashed after her.

"Goodbye, Bolt," Linda yelled.

Bolt heard the front door open and then slam shut. He stopped where he was, halfway across the living room that led to the vestibule.

"Damn!" he said out loud. He buried his head in his hands, rubbed his forehead with his fingers, and felt a knot of tension grip his stomach.

He sighed and turned around, knowing that there was no way of persuading Linda to come back. Once she made up her mind to something, she was the stubbornest woman in the world.

Before he got back to the kitchen, he heard the back door open and close. He figured it was either Harmony or Clarissa, returning to clean up the mess from the beans.

"I'm in here," he called from the living room, already heading toward the kitchen.

"And I'm in here," Tom answered from the back door entrance room.

"Damn you, Tom," Bolt yelled when he dashed into the kitchen. "What in the hell do you think you're doing, you scumball traitor. Why in the hell did you let Linda go?"

Tom held up both hands and tucked his head down into his neck. "Hold it. Wait a minute, Bolt. What in the hell are you attacking me for?"

"Because you let her go over to The Proud Peacock, you dirty bastard." Enraged, Bolt drew back his fist, started to swing.

Tom reached out and blocked Bolt's arm. "I didn't let her do shit. She did it on her own."

"You helped her, you sonofabitch," Bolt shouted, shaking his fist in Tom's face. "You sneaked her horse up to the front yard so she could get away before I could stop her."

"Now wait just a damned minute, Bolt. I brought her horse up here as a favor to her. I thought you knew she was going over there."

"How in the hell would I know? I've been gone all morning, getting my ass shot at."

"All right, calm down, Bolt. You know there's no stopping Linda once she's got her mind made

174

up to something. We can't stop her from going over to The Proud Peacock. Neither one of us."

Bolt lowered his head, brought his arm down. "I know it, dammit, but she's gonna get hurt over there."

"Maybe not, Bolt. Linda's pretty shrewd. And, quite frankly, I thought her idea of working as a whore so she could spy on them was pretty damned good."

"Aw, shit, Tom. What are we gonna do?" Bolt pulled a chair out from the table and plunked down in it. He shook his head and tried to think.

"Pray that Linda can get Doris to come back and at the same time find out what happened to Clarissa's brother."

"Yeah, I guess you're right."

Tom pulled out another chair and sat down across the table from Bolt. He pushed the mess from the beans aside. "What did you mean you got your ass shot at?" he asked.

"Yeah. Lyle Watley knows we're checking up on him. He sent his henchman after me to take me out." He told Tom the gory details of the ambush. "That's why I'm dead set against Linda going over there. If they find out what she's up to, they'll kill her for sure, and they won't even have to hunt her down."

"Jeez, Bolt, I didn't know it was this serious. What in the hell do you think they're doing over there? Killing their customers? Kidnapping them?"

"I don't know, but we'd damned sure better find out in a hurry," Bolt said. "Tom, you've got to go

175

over there tonight and check it out."

"Thanks a lot, Bolt," Tom said sarcastically. "You get your ass shot at today and now you expect me to ride over there and pretend to be a customer. They may be dumb, but they're not stupid. They'd blow me away before I got my foot inside the door."

"You can handle it, Tom. If Linda can pull it off, so can you."

"She can do it a hell of a lot easier than I could," Tom said. "Jessie Belle knows we're partners and that isn't gonna smell right to her if I suddenly show up wanting to spend time with one of her whores. Especially now that they know we're checking up on them."

"Just tell her that you and I had a big fight or something, if she asks."

"Hell, no. I already told you I ain't doin' you no more favors."

"But, Tom, we've got Linda and Doris to think about. And Clarissa's brother."

"Oh, yes. Clarissa. Dammit, Bolt, every fuckin' time you fall in love, I'm the one who ends up in danger."

"Listen, Tom, I think these missing men are being drugged. I think someone's slipping something into their drinks. We've got to find out where Jessie and her men are taking these fellows, and why."

"Do you suppose they're taking them somewhere and killing them?" Tom asked.

"I don't think so. Most of them are drifters, with no money, or drovers who haven't been paid yet. There's got to be another explanation."

"None of it makes sense," Tom said.

"That's why you've got to get in there somehow and find out what's going on," Bolt said.

"And how would I do that?"

"I've got an idea, Tom. Hire on as a helper. That way you'd get in on the bottom floor of their operation."

"You really think Jezebel would hire me? Come on, Bolt. I think you've finally lost your mind."

"It could work, Tom. Just tell Jessie that you and I came to blows and that the partnership is over between us. Tell her you want to get even with me and that you know it will hurt me more than anything else if I find out you're working for her."

"And you really think she'd buy that line of shit?" Tom said as he shook his head.

Bolt knew Tom was weakening.

"Please, Tom, you've got to do this favor for me," he pleaded.

Tom hesitated, then looked at Bolt.

"All right, Bolt. I'll do it. I'll go over there tonight and see what I can find out."

Bolt sighed.

"Oh, thank you, Tom. You don't know what this means to me. If you were a woman, I'd kiss you."

"Then, thank God I'm not. And I want to make one thing clear from the start."

"What's that, Tom?"

"I'm doing this for Linda's sake, sure as hell not for yours."

"That's fine with me, Tom. And I don't suppose you'll be too upset if you have to sleep with one of Jessie's whores, just to keep them from becoming suspicious about you, you understand."

"No, Bolt. Just so I don't have to sleep with Jessie, I wouldn't mind that at all."

# CHAPTER FIFTEEN

Linda Ramsey paused in front of the door of
The Proud Peacock and took a deep breath. It
was two o'clock on a Friday afternoon, not a
particularly busy time for most whorehouses.
Still, she was surprised that there were only four
horses tied up at the hitchrails, including her
own. From what she'd heard about the new
whorehouse, she had assumed that it was over-
flowing with customers at all hours of the day
and night.

As she stood at the front door, she heard very
little noise from inside. Low murmurs of conversation and an occasional burst of laughter.

She was glad she'd chosen to wear her plain,
sandy-brown dress with its chocolate-colored pip-
ing and long, flared skirt. It was simple enough
that it wouldn't draw attention to her and yet
tight enough in the right places to show her large
breasts off to her advantage.

If she had chosen one of her skimpy harlot costumes instead, she would have been too obvious in her ploy to get a job at the new whorehouse, and she might have aroused Jessie Belle's suspicions right away.

As it was, she hoped she could carry out her scheme without getting found out.

She squared her shoulders, fluffed her blond hair, and opened the door. She paused again just inside the door, and glanced around the massive room. There were only four people in the room, six, if she counted herself and the short, stubby bartender. A dusky-skinned harlot sat on the long couch between two men. The man who had his arm around the harlot was obviously a customer and the other fellow sat farther away from the girl, but joined in the conversation. Another fellow sat on a bar stool, talking to the bartender.

Jessie Belle was nowhere in sight. Neither was Doris Fletcher.

Linda strolled over to the bar, her carpetbag clutched in her hand.

"Can I help you, ma'am?" asked the balding bartender. He was not the same man who tended bar on the opening night celebration. As far as she could remember, the other barkeep had been slender and had dark hair. She remembered the red bandanna he had worn around his neck, and the beautiful leather vest.

It didn't matter, she thought. A bartender couldn't be expected to be on duty twenty-four hours a day and she figured the more handsome bartender worked at night.

"Yes, I'm looking for Miss Jessie Belle," Linda said.

The barkeep looked her over, settled his gaze on the mounds of her breasts.

"Are you looking for a job?"

"Yes, sir."

"Ernie, take the lady to Jessie's office."

The dark-complexioned man slid off the stool and walked with a limp as he escorted her to a small office in a hallway beyond the staircase. He knocked on the open door. "Someone to see you, Miss Belle," he said, then turned and limped away.

Jessie looked up when Linda entered the room.

"Hello, I'm Linda Ramsey and I'm looking for a job as a prostitute."

Jessie's eyes narrowed suspiciously as she looked Linda over. "You're one of Bolt's whores, aren't you?"

"I *was*," Linda said. "I quit this morning."

"Why?"

"For several reasons, but mainly because I asked for more money and he said no. That day you came over to the Rocking Bar to recruit more prostitutes, you made us a good offer and I decided to take you up on it."

"What are the other reasons you quit?"

Linda set her carpetbag down on the floor beside her. "Bolt demanded too much of us. He

181

yelled at us all the time. He forced me to go to bed with him whenever he had the whim, whether it was in the middle of the night or five o'clock in the morning."

"Bolt told me he didn't sleep with his whores," Jessie said, her eyes narrowing to slits.

"Bolt says a lot of things that aren't true. He always promised us spending money, but we very seldom got it. Yes, he gave us a place to sleep and put food on our table, but he paid us so little, we couldn't even buy new costumes. And since you opened up, our business has dropped off to nothing. Bolt told us this morning that from now on, he would pay us only for the actual time we spent with our legs spread. Which is almost nothing. That's when I quit."

"I don't believe you, Miss Ramsey." Jessie said, her expression cold and hard.

"I'm not asking you to, Miss Belle. I'm asking for a job." Linda's knees were shaking beneath her skirt and she hoped her nervousness didn't show.

"I think Bolt sent you over here to spy on me."

"Thank you for your time, Miss Belle," Linda said as she picked up her carpetbag. "I don't choose to work for someone who is suspicious. I had enough of that when I worked for Bolt."

"Just a minute, Linda. Perhaps I'm being too hasty in my judgment of you."

"Look, Miss Belle, I don't need your damned job," Linda said, clutching her carpetbag tightly so the trembling in her hands wouldn't show. "I've been in the business long enough to know all the tricks and I can get a job in any whorehouse across the land. In fact, I've been thinking about opening my own brothel in town."

"I don't think you'd have much luck. It takes money to open a whorehouse, Linda."

Linda saw the gloat on Jessie's face. "Not much, the way I see it."

"And how's that?"

"I figured I could rent a little room near the stockyards and it would be a one-woman operation until I got on my feet. Can you imagine how much money I could make servicing all those randy drovers when they come in off the trail?" Linda saw Jessie's eyes widen, her mouth fall slack, and knew she'd struck a sensitive chord.

"Sit down, Linda."

Linda didn't. "No, Miss Belle. I sense your hostility toward me and I think I'd be better off working for myself."

"I remember you now," Jessie said with a nervous smile. "On my opening night, you're the whore who refused to turn around so I could look you over."

"That's right, Miss Belle," Linda said boldly. "If I'm getting paid for it, I do what I'm told. If I'm not, I do what I want."

"I like your spunk, Linda. Tell me, why would you want to work here when you know how badly Abby was hurt?"

"It was an unfortunate incident, Miss Belle. Sometimes customers get drunk and sometimes they get rough. I'm used to that and it doesn't bother me any more. Abby was too new at the job to understand how men are. But I've been spreading my legs long enough to know how to handle the rough stuff."

"But sometimes men get rough on purpose, not just because they're mean drunks," Jessie said. "If you know what I mean."

"Oh, I know that," Linda said, tossing it off lightly.

Jessie sat forward in her chair. "If you work for me, you'll have to go along with whatever the men want you to do because that's how we're able to attract so much business."

"I understand that," Linda said as she lowered her carpetbag to the floor again.

"Here at The Proud Peacock, we promise our customers any type of sex they want. I've done it before so I know it's pretty hard to stomach sometimes, but we give them what they want. The more bizarre the sexual act, the more we charge them for it. And believe me, we're making a small fortune on the quirks of these men with sick minds."

"I believe you."

"Are you still interested in working here, Linda?" Jessie asked. "I can offer you twenty-five dollars a week, plus room and board."

"I don't know, Miss Belle. If I worked for

myself, I could make a lot more money," Linda said as she looked Jessie directly in the eye. "At two dollars a crack, I could make a hundred and fifty a week off those drovers without even trying."

"Well, I certainly couldn't pay you that much, but I could give you fifty a week."

"Well, maybe I'll try it for awhile," Linda said. "When do I start?"

"Right now," Jessie said. "Just as soon as you change your clothes."

Linda heaved a sigh of relief. She hoped Jessie hadn't heard it.


Tom Penrod strolled into the crowded whorehouse that night like he owned the place. Lyle Watley stepped up to relieve him of his weapon and his hat. Tom waved him off and walked straight to the bar without looking around the room first.

He elbowed his way through a cluster of men and stepped up to the bar.

"Whiskey," he told the heavy-set bartender. He glanced at the others lining the bar and saw Brutus glaring at him from the far end. When the barkeep set the drink down in front of him, he upended the tumbler and drank it down in one gulp. "Another," he said.

When the second drink was served, Tom fished a coin out of his pocket, slid it across the counter and walked away with the glass in his hand. He threaded his way across the room and didn't see any of the harlots. When he spotted Jessie talking to one of the men, he walked over close enough to be noticed by her without being obvious about it. He knew he was being closely watched by both Watley and Brutus.

Jessie had a startled expression on her face when she glanced up and saw him. Tom looked the other way.

"Did Bolt send you over to check on us?" she said as she walked up to him.

"Don't mention his name," Tom snapped. He took a sip of the whiskey.

"What's the matter? You and your friend have a misunderstanding?"

"Worse than that, but it's none of your concern. I came here to get laid." He tipped the glass up again, but barely wet his lips with it.

"Well, I'm sure we can accommodate you, Mister Penrod."

"It's just Tom, unless you want me to call you ma'am," he said with an angry snarl.

Jessie laughed haughtily and Tom wanted to punch her in the face. "Just call me Jessie," she said. "You're in a foul mood tonight."

"With good reason."

"Let's go over in the corner where it's quiet," Jessie suggested. "You need to calm down."

Tom followed her over to a small square table near the front of the room. Four men were already

186

sitting there but when they saw Jessie, they got up and offered her the table.

"Would you like to talk about it?" she said after they sat down.

Tom knew that she didn't give a damn about him or anyone else. The redheaded bitch was just prying for information.

"Only two things I want to do tonight. I want to get laid and I want to get rip-roaring drunk. Who's the best whore you've got here?"

"Maria. But she's going to be busy for quite some time. You'd have a long wait."

Again, Tom tipped the drink to his lips, pretending to drink. "Is she worth waiting for?"

"Most men think so. That's why she's so busy."

"Then I'll wait." Tom took a real sip of the whiskey and glanced around the room, making note of the clientele The Proud Peacock drew. In general it was a much rougher crowd than they had at the Rocking Bar. There were very few businessmen. Many of the men looked like drovers, but there were enough of them who looked like outlaws to make Tom uncomfortable.

"You heard that Linda Ramsey came to work for me today," Jessie said.

"I don't blame her. I wouldn't be surprised if a couple more of our harlots came looking for a job."

"It's that bad over there?" Jessie asked.

"I don't want to talk about it." Tom glanced around the room, hoping to spot Doris and Linda when they came downstairs. He turned back to Jessie and forced a smile. "This might not be a bad place to work."

"You looking for a job, Tom?"

"Not yet, but I'm thinking about making a move real soon."

"There's Linda. I need to talk to her. Would you excuse me for a minute?"

As Jessie left the table, Tom glanced across the room and saw Linda coming down the stairs. Jessie caught up with Linda in the middle of the room and Tom got up and walked over within hearing distance.

"No, I won't do it," Linda said.

"You have to do it, Linda. You're working for me now and you'll do as I say."

"Well, you can't make me do it," Linda shouted. "It's too obscene, too brutal."

"We have our ways," Jessie said, her eyes full of hatred.

Some of the men in the room started to gather around them in a big circle. Tom noticed Brutus lumbering over from the bar.

"How much extra would you pay me?" Linda asked.

"Not a damned penny," Jessie said. "It's part of your job."

"Bullshit! You told me that you charged extra for such gross acts of perversion," Linda cried. "I want my cut."

Tom figured that Linda was causing a scene on

188

purpose and he was proud of her.

"Quiet, Linda. We do charge extra," Jessie said in a hushed voice, "but you're getting paid for your services and this is your duty."

"You're nothing but a greedy bitch as far as I'm concerned," Linda shouted. "You charge your customers a lot of money and you can't even toss your whores a small crumb."

"Hush, you ungrateful slut!" Jessie slapped Linda hard across the face.

"How dare you, you filthy bitch." Linda doubled up her fist and socked Jessie in the stomach.

Tom moved closer for a better look. Others stepped back to give the girls room as cheers rose up from the men.

Jessie reached out and grabbed Linda's hand, raked her fingernails across the flesh, drawing blood.

Linda kicked Jessie in the shins, then grabbed a hank of her red hair and tugged on it until Jessie's head was tipped way back. Jessie screamed as Linda continued to jerk her hair, bobbing Jessie's head up and down.

Brutus, who was twice as big as both girls put together, moved into the circle of space around the girls. He grabbed Linda from behind, tore her away from Jessie. He picked her up with both hands and bounced her up and down on the floor.

Tom's anger flared up. One girl against another girl was a fair fight, but when you added a man the size of Brutus, the fight became very lopsided.

Tom stepped into the circle and took Brutus on. He punched the giant in the side, trying to force him to release Linda. The hard blow to the big man barely fazed him. Tom jammed his elbow into the brute's rib cage.

Brutus groaned with the pain and let Linda go. He swung on Tom and bloodied his chin.

Tom kicked the big man in the balls. Brutus doubled over in pain. Tom snatched his pistol from the holster, flipped it around so he held it by the barrel. He swung it high in the air, ready to crack Brutus' skull with the butt end.

Jessie pulled a derringer out of her skirt pocket, aimed at Tom. She pulled the trigger, missed her shot as the bullet sang on by him and thunked into the wall behind him.

Linda stepped in and knocked the gun out of Jessie's hand before she could fire another shot. The two girls got into it again, pulling hair, scratching and trying to pluck each other's eyeballs out.

Brutus came after Tom again, punched him on both sides of his body at the same time. Tom managed another boot to the big man's groin. When Brutus doubled over, Tom slammed the butt of his pistol into the man's skull. Brutus toppled to the floor with a thud as loud as a felled tree.

Tom scrambled over and separated the brawling girls, dragged them to a corner of the room.

"If you two want to fight like men, you'd better step outside."

He whirled around and marched toward the door, amidst a round of cheers from the crowd. Outside, he wiped the blood from his mouth, then mounted his horse, aching in every muscle.

By the time he got home, after a five-minute ride, he was in a violent rage. He hurt so bad, he didn't even take his horse down to the stable. He tied it to the front porch and stalked inside. He found Bolt and Harmony in the kitchen.

"What happened to you, Tom?" Bolt said as he jumped up.

Harmony got up and reached for the water bowl and a fresh towel.

"I ain't gonna tangle with Brutus again just to get a fuckin' job," he roared. "Next time, Bolt, you do your own damned dirty work."

# CHAPTER SIXTEEN

"I don't know what we're going to do," Bolt told Harmony over breakfast the following morning. "Tom refuses to go back over to The Proud Peacock. I can't really blame him, but he's our only hope."

"Did you hear that, Bolt?"

"What?"

Harmony tilted her head and listened. "I guess not. I thought I heard a knock at the front door."

"I'll check it," Bolt said. Harmony followed him into the entrance hall, where he pulled the curtain aside and looked outside. He saw nothing unusual in the early morning dawn. He slid the bolt across and opened the door slowly.

He was stunned when he saw Doris Fletcher lying on the porch, her body wrapped in a dark blanket. Her eyes were closed and her face was so bruised he hardly recognized her.

"Oh, my God," Harmony cried as they both knelt down beside Doris.

Bolt thought the girl was dead at first, but when he felt her inner wrist, he found a weak pulse.

"She's still alive," Bolt said. "Let's get her inside."

He scooped her up in his arms and carried her inside, took her to his bedroom and gently placed her on his bed.

"Get a wet cloth," Harmony said as she stripped the blanket away from Doris. She unbuttoned the girl's robe and gasped when she pulled it open.

"What's the matter?" Bolt said as he dashed over from the dresser, a wet cloth in his hand. He shook his head when he saw the cuts and bruises that covered almost every inch of Doris' body.

"That poor girl," Harmony said. "I don't think she's going to make it, Bolt. Here, hold this cloth on her forehead."

While Harmony ran to the kitchen to get the tray of medicines, Bolt stood over the bed, and got sick to his stomach when he looked at the bruises. When Harmony returned a couple of minutes later, she set the tray down on the nightstand and began the tedious job of examining each and every wound.

"What's all the commotion?" Tom said as he limped into the room. He walked over and looked down at the bed. "Jeez, what happened?"

"I wish to hell I knew," Bolt said. "Did you see Doris when you were over at The Proud Peacock last night?"

"No. I didn't see any of the girls except Linda."

"Was she all right?"

"She was when I left, except for a few scratches," Tom said. "I have a feeling this has something to do with the fight she staged with Jessie."

"We've got to get Linda out of there," Bolt said.

Doris' eyelids fluttered open. "Bolt?" she said in a voice so weak, he could hardly hear her.

"We're here," said Bolt as he took her hand. "You're going to be all right."

"Can you talk, Doris?" Harmony asked.

"Yes," she answered weakly.

"What happened?" Harmony said. She pulled the blanket over Doris.

"Two men did it." Doris licked her dry lips.

"With whips?" Bolt asked.

"Whips, knives, bondage, torture, other things." Each word was an effort.

"Don't talk any more," Harmony said. "We'll take care of you."

"Boat," Doris said in a dry rasp.

"Yes, I'm here, Doris," Bolt said.

"Boat . . . boat," she said again.

"Boat?" Bolt asked.

The sick girl nodded her head slightly.

"They were going to take you on a boat?" Bolt asked. He leaned down close to her face so he could hear her.

"Yes . . . Linda . . . help . . . me . . . escape."

"So that's why Linda started the fight," Tom said. "To distract everyone."

Doris nodded her head.

"Where were they going to take you on the

194

boat?" Bolt asked.

"Don't . . . know . . ." And then her eyes closed as she slipped back into unconsciousness.

"Well, I'm surprised to see you here," Jessie Belle said when Tom walked into The Proud Peacock that night.

Tom was surprised, too, because he had vowed that he'd never set foot in the place again. But after Doris came home all battered up, he knew he had to get Linda out of there before she was killed. And they were still looking for Clarissa's brother.

Doris had slipped in and out of consciousness enough during the day that she had been able to provide them with more information. She said that after the two customers had tortured her and bruised her so badly, Jessie was afraid that she would go back to the Rocking Bar Ranch where Bolt would see her. So she was held prisoner in a locked room until they could take her away to meet a boat.

Doris also told them that she remembered Randy Mayfield. He had been her customer but he had gotten very drunk and passed out before they could do anything. Lyle Watley and another man had carried Randy out of her room. She had mentioned that she had heard a wagon leaving that same night, sometime after midnight.

"I came over to apologize to you for last night," Tom said.

"It was a bad day all around," Jessie said. "I'll

forget about it if you do."

"Except for the soreness, it's forgotten. How's Linda doing?"

"She's fine. We came to an agreement about the money and she's going to stay on."

"Good. She's a good whore."

"I suppose you and Bolt patched things up between you," she said.

Tom knew she was fishing for information. "As you said, it was a bad day all around. I'm on my way to town now to see if I can find another job."

"What happened between you?"

"It's something I'd rather not discuss in public." Tom nodded toward the clusters of noisy customers.

"Why don't we walk over to my little log cabin where we can be alone?"

Tom saw the hint of suggestion in her eyes. "I'm not sure I could trust myself."

"What do you mean?" Jessie said with a mild flirtation.

"Being alone with a pretty young lady might get us both in trouble."

"It just might," Jessie said, a playful smile on her face.

"Jessie, you're not flirting with me, are you?" he grinned.

"That's for me to know."

She led him over to the log cabin where Lem Campbell's caretaker had lived for a few years.

"Now, what about Bolt?" she asked as soon as she closed the door.

"He's a damned thief. Besides not paying me

much for my work, he's been stealing money from both businesses. The cattle and the bordello."

"But I thought you two were partners."

"I thought so, too, until I discovered all that money missing. But I don't want to talk about him when I'm in the company of a beautiful woman." Tom leaned over and kissed Jessie tenderly on the cheek, ran his lips up the side of her face to her forehead.

Jessie shuddered. "I'll bet you're a better lover than Bolt," she said in a husky voice.

"I wouldn't know about that, Jessie." He kissed her on the neck and made her shudder again.

"What's he like around the harlots?" she cooed.

"Not very pleasant. He yells at them a lot, bats 'em around if they give him any guff. But they're whores. What do you expect?"

"Bolt said he treated his whores real special. He bragged about how good he was to them," she said as she thrust her body up against his.

"What do you expect him to say? That he beats them on a regular basis?" Tom found her lips and kissed her hard, sliding his tongue into her wet mouth.

"You know what I think, Tom?" she husked as she drew her lips away from his.

"No."

"I think you're a liar."

Tom backed up and looked down at the short woman. "You got a funny way of being romantic," he said.

"I think Bolt sent you over here to watch over Linda."

"Are you talking about last night? Bolt had nothing to do with that. Hell, I was just protecting Linda."

"I know you were, but I think you were doing it for Bolt."

"Shit, Bolt didn't even know I was over here last night. He'd have cut off my balls if he had known."

"That's funny."

"Not to me, it ain't. Look, Jessie, I ain't much on chivalry. I sleep with whores where such things don't matter. Hell, I don't have to be polite to them. I just go in and get my rocks off and leave."

"Linda's a whore, and you stood up for her like a gentleman."

"Shit, I couldn't just stand by and watch Brutus attacking Linda like that. It was an unfair fight. Linda can take care of herself pretty well, but you got to admit that she was at a hell of a disadvantage with that big gorilla. Hell, he could've picked her up with one hand and crushed her to death without even half trying."

"Yes, he's strong enough to do it," Jessie said as she stood on tiptoes and kissed Tom's mouth. "That's why I hired him as a bouncer."

Tom thought he was getting through to Jessie. Not only was he putting Bolt down real good, he was putting down the whores because he knew how little she respected them. If he worked it right, he'd wangle that job out of her.

"You're such a pretty young thing," he said as he took her in his arms and drew her tight. He kissed her deep and pressed his beginning hardness against her.

"What would Bolt say if he could see you now?" she said as she wiggled up against him.

"He'd probably kill me," Tom husked. "But I don't care. One night with you would be worth it."

"If you really want me, you'll have to prove yourself to me."

"What do you mean?"

"You'll have to kill Bolt."

Tom was dumbfounded. He hadn't counted on this complication. "That seems a little severe."

"That's what I thought," she said as she stepped away from him. "You and Bolt are in this together. You don't hate him at all."

"That's not true, Jessie. I'd gladly kill Bolt, but if I do, I'll face jail and probably death by hanging. He isn't worth it."

"I'll add a little extra incentive," Jessie said.

"Like what?"

"I'll give you a job, Tom."

"What kind of a job?"

"I need a new bartender," Jessie said.

"A bartender," Tom laughed. "You expect me to kill Bolt for a job as a bartender?"

"It would only be for a little while, Tom. Just until we can find a replacement for Rodney Abel, who died yesterday afternoon."

"I'm sorry, Jessie. I didn't know that you'd lost one of your employees yesterday. You should have said something."

"I'm very saddened by Rodney's tragic death, but we have to go on with life."

"How'd he die?"

"His horse broke a leg and threw him. Unfortunately for Rodney, he happened to be carrying a sharp dagger in his hand at the time. When he landed on the ground, the dagger went straight through his heart. He died instantly."

"Where'd it happen?"

"Oddly enough, the accident occurred right around the bend from here. Lyle discovered the body when he came home from town."

Tom had the feeling that there was something phony about her story. After all, who carries a sharp dagger in his hand when he's riding?

"That's terrible, Jessie."

"Yes. And even more tragic because Rodney didn't have any family except a sister named Annie who lives up in Austin. We had no way to let her know about her brother's death, so we buried Rodney this morning in the small cemetery in San Antonio. We'll get over it."

"Well, I'm sorry."

"You can see that we need a bartender. Ollie's filling in for now, but he's in such poor health, I'm afraid he'll drop dead of a heart attack."

"I understand, Jessie, but I really don't want to be a bartender. I'm an outdoor boy and I couldn't stand to be cooped up behind a bar all day."

"Then I've got something else in mind for you," Tom. Something very special."

"Doing what?" Tom asked.

"I can't tell you that until after Bolt is dead, but it's something that will bring you a lot of money. You'll be working with Lyle Watley, who is the only person I trust. That should prove how I feel about you. Now I want you to prove yourself to me."

"Will you let me make love to you?"

"Yes. Just as soon as Bolt is dead."

"You're asking a lot of me, Jessie."

"I'm worth it, Tom. And you'll find out for yourself just as soon as Bolt is dead."

"I'll do it, Jessie. For you, I'll risk my own neck."

# CHAPTER SEVENTEEN

"We'll do it, Tom," Bolt said the next morning after Tom told him what Jessie Belle wanted him to do. Bolt flexed his stiff muscles. He had slept on the couch the night before. Doris Fletcher was better, but she'd been too sick to move from Bolt's bed.

"You want me to kill you?" Tom said.

"If that's what it takes. I have a feeling that we're getting very close to solving this thing. You've got to get that job with her, at all costs."

"Choose your death," Tom laughed. "Dueling sword. Shotgun to the head. Drowning. Burning. I can think of a dozen ways to do you in."

"I think you've just hit on something, Tom."

"What's that?"

"I think I should die in a fire. Not so messy, and not so many remains to identify."

"I see what you mean, Bolt. You burn up and there's not enough of you left that Jessie can prove if it's you, one way or the other."

"Yes, Tom. Now all we have to do is decide when and where. It's Sunday, a good day to die. After supper, of course," he added.

After discussing several options, they decided

that Bolt's mock death would take place that night, shortly after dark, in the abandoned shack that stood at the edge of their property, on the back forty. There would be a memorial service Monday morning and everyone would be invited but Bolt.

They kept their plan secret from everyone but Clarissa Mayfield. They would need her help if they were going to carry out their plan.

Bolt and Tom spent a good part of the day getting ready for Bolt's death. They rode out to the abandoned shack and stuffed it with as many dead leaves and twigs as they could gather up. They set other things out in the stable so they could take them to the shack when they needed them.

Clarissa had the hardest part, and yet it was the easiest. All she had to do was to take the buckboard to San Antonio and convince the undertaker that she was the grieving sister of Rodney Abel, the poor soul who was laid to rest the previous morning. And once that was accomplished, she had only to convince the undertaker to dig up the remains so they could be buried in the family plot in Austin.

If she got the remains, she was to head north and meet Tom at a certain spot and he would handle it from there. Clarissa would then check into a hotel and wait for Bolt to join her.

When Tom had told him about Rodney Abel, Bolt knew that Abel was the one who had tried to ambush him two days before. Rodney Abel was the man Bolt had shot in the chest to save his own life. To Bolt, it was ironic justice. Abel would die again. And again, it would be to save Bolt's life.

Bolt enjoyed Sunday supper more than any he'd had in a long time. They ate early that day, well before dark. They all ate in the big ranch house because Doris was still using Bolt's bed for her recovery.

Everything was set for the fireworks that evening. The body of Rodney Abel rested in the shack, covered by dried leaves. The body had been dressed in Bolt's clothing, including a pair of old boots that Bolt used when he went fishing, and Bolt's belt, complete with its fancy gold belt buckle that bore his initials in raised letters. The belt buckle was the item they hoped would survive the fire enough to be recognized.

Clarissa Mayfield said goodbye to her new friends shortly after supper, telling them that she wanted to ride back home just in case, by some miracle, Randy had returned to the ranch.

Clarissa left the house and rode toward town, where she would stop at the hotel.

A few minutes after Clarissa left, Bolt announced that he was going to spend the night in his fishing shack so that he could walk down to the river before dawn and catch breakfast for everyone. He joked about it, saying he'd rather sleep on the hard ground inside the shack than to spend another night on that damned lumpy couch in the living room.

Bolt left the house and rode toward the fishing shack until he was out of sight of the house. Then he angled south and rode through the woods toward San Antonio, where he would meet Clarissa at the hotel.

And some time after Bolt left, when it was almost dark, Tom told the girls that he was going to ride over to The Proud Peacock and check on Linda Ramsey.

Tom rode toward the fishing shack where he would start a small fire inside the shack before he rode to The Proud Peacock.

"Could we talk privately?" Tom asked Jessie Belle when she greeted him inside The Proud Peacock.

Jessie gave him a questioning look. "Do you have news for me?"

"I've come to apply for a job," Tom said. "And to collect my reward."

Jessie smiled, but it was a smile of relief, not one of happiness, Tom thought.

"Let's go to my cabin," she said. "I'll take a bottle of my best brandy for the celebration."

When Jessie walked over to the bar, Tom scanned the crowded room, frantically searching for Linda. He had the feeling that things were about to explode and he wanted her out of there tonight. In fact, he wasn't sure but what he would be walking into a trap himself tonight.

He saw one of the dusky-skinned harlots coming down the stairs, but there was no sign of

Linda. He glanced around for something to scribble a note on, but saw nothing. He was just about to walk over to the harlot to give her a message for Linda when he saw Jessie coming back from the bar, a full bottle of brandy in her hands.

They didn't talk until they were well inside the log cabin, which was lit by a burning lantern.

Jessie got two brandy snifters from the china cabinet and asked Tom to open the bottle. Tom opened the bottle, sniffed the cork, then poured a small amount of the amber liquid into each glass. He picked up both glasses, handed one of them to Jessie.

"Did you take care of Bolt?" she asked.

"Yes, Jessie. Just before I rode over here. He's gone now. And as far as I'm concerned, the bastard got just what he deserved."

Jessie eyed him suspiciously.

"How can I be sure he's dead?"

"You can take my word for it, or if you want, I can take you to see the grisly remains."

"Not tonight," she said. "But you can be sure I'll have one of my men check it out."

"I figured you wouldn't take my word for it. I've planned a memorial service for Bolt in the morning, over at the Rocking Bar. You or your men are welcome to inspect the remains before the burial."

"Someone will be there," she said.

"Good. I hope you'll come and pay your respects to the girls. They're going to be very upset over this."

"Perhaps I will come over."

"I know Linda and Doris work for you now, but

I think it would be nice if they came to the memorial service, too."

He saw Jessie's eyes widen in surprise.

"Doris doesn't work for me any more."

"Oh, I didn't know that. Do you know where she is? I'd like to let her know about Bolt."

"I don't know. I thought she'd gone back to your place."

"Well, maybe someone will know where she is."

Jessie raised her brandy glass in the air. "To Bolt's memory," she said.

"May it live forever," Tom added as he clinked his glass against hers. "Good brandy," he said after he took a sip.

"The best," she said as she took a drink.

"When do I start work, Jessie?"

"Tonight if you want to."

"Oh?"

"You can tend bar until midnight, when the new man comes on."

Tom frowned. "I thought you said I'd be doing something special."

Jessie laughed. "You will be, but Ollie isn't feeling well tonight and I thought as long as you're here, you wouldn't mind pouring a few drinks."

"I guess I could do that."

"Seriously, Tom, starting tomorrow, you will be expected to move over here to The Proud Peacock. After the memorial services, of course. You'll sleep in the bunkhouse with my other employees."

"I thought maybe since Bolt was gone now, I'd

stay over at the Rocking Bar and ride over here when I'm working. At least until I can sell the ranch."

"No, it wouldn't work that way. You have to be here all the time because with the type of work you'll be doing, you have to be prepared to leave with Lyle at a minute's notice."

"You've got me curious now," he said.

"Lyle will explain the details when the time is right, but I know you'll be leaving on your first trip tomorrow night. About midnight. I'm telling you just so you'll be prepared."

"Midnight?"

"Yes, Lyle likes to ride at night. It's cooler for the horses pulling the wagons."

"Do you know where we're going?"

"I guess it won't hurt to tell you that. You'll take the wagons to Corpus Christi where you'll meet a boat. Then you'll turn around and come back."

"Are you bringing supplies in, or shipping them out?" Tom laughed.

"Lyle will explain everything after the wagons pull out." She set her glass down on the table and began unbuttoning the front of her dress. "Are you ready for your reward, Tom?"

"I thought you'd never ask."

Jessie took his glass from him, set it down next to hers, then took his hand and led him into her feminine bedroom.

"Hurry and get undressed," she said. "Being modest, I'll undress behind my screen." She smiled sensually, then ducked behind the three-paneled screen that was painted with Chinese designs.

Tom unbuttoned his shirt as he walked across the room and tossed it on a chair near the dresser. As he was unbuckling his belt, he noticed the bottle behind the water pitcher. The label said: CHLORAL HYDRATE. Knockout drops, he thought.

Suddenly the puzzle was beginning to come together. And Tom knew what the wagon cargo would be. Drugged cattle drovers, and drifters. Men who wouldn't be missed if they turned up missing.

Where would the boat take these drugged men? And why?

# CHAPTER EIGHTEEN

"How do I look?" Bolt asked as he paraded around the hotel room in the colorful Mexican serape and the floppy sombrero Clarissa had bought for his disguise. She sat on the edge of the bed, barefooted, her own shawl-like serape draped around her shoulders. Her smaller sombrero sat on the dresser next to the water pitcher and bowl.

"Like a peasant right out of the fields," she laughed.

Bolt walked over to the dressing table, bent down to look in the mirror. He pulled the hat forward slightly so the wide brim hid his forehead.

"I hope this works, Clarissa," he said with his back to her. "I don't want Watley to recognize me at the last minute and mess everything up."

"Do you think we'll find my brother down there?" she asked as she stood up.

"I'm counting on it."

Clarissa pulled the serape open and let it fall on the bed behind her. She wore only the black, filmy nightgown she'd borrowed from Cathy Boring.

"And how do I look?" she said, a sudden husk to her voice.

Bolt bent lower and glanced at her reflection in the mirror. Startled, he looked closer, then whirled around to face her.

She smiled coyly.

"You look . . . beautiful, Clarissa," he said as he stared at the fullness of her breasts beneath the sheer material.

Clarissa bent over and grabbed the bottom of the gown, pulled it slowly up her legs, exposing her trim ankles first, then the smooth flesh of her lower legs.

Bolt stood there in stunned silence as she drew the gown up to her knees, her thighs. She hesitated as the bottom of the gown reached the Y of her legs and Bolt saw only a hint of her furry sex.

"Do you know what you're doing, Clarissa?" he said as the heat of desire flooded his loins and caused his stalk to swell.

"I hope so," she said, her eyes glazed with desire. "I figured neither one of us wanted to sleep on the floor tonight."

She drew the gown up more so that the triangle of her sex was fully visible, then her flat tummy, and finally her swollen breasts. She tugged the gown up over her head and it floated to the floor in a soft rustle of cloth.

"Clarissa, don't tease me like this."

"I'm not teasing," she said, her voice filled with velvet seduction.

"Please, Clarissa," he said as he started toward the bed, his voice cracking with desire. "Don't do this unless you're sure."

"I'm sure."

Bolt sat on an old crate near the large expanse of blue water and watched the bustle of activity as the sailors prepared to sail. At his feet, Clarissa sat on a blanket that she'd spread out on the sand. Off to their right, the land of Corpus Christi curved out to the sea.

Dressed in their Mexican garb, they had been there all morning, watching the gently bobbing boat, squinting against the sun when they looked out at the white, rolling waves, checking the road behind them for some sign of the covered wagon that would bring Tom and Lyle Watley and Watley's prisoners to this remote seaside port. Their own carriage was tied up near the scattering of buildings that made up the town of Corpus Christi.

Bolt reached inside the serape and patted the holstered pistol. He wore a matching weapon on the other side and Clarissa carried a small derringer in the pocket of her long brown skirt.

He turned his head when he heard the rumbling

of wagon wheels in the distance and saw the wagon with two men perched in the driver's seat.

"Here they come," he said. "Are you ready?"

Clarissa nodded. She stood up, shook the sand from the blanket, folded it and stuffed it into the big pouch purse she carried.

Bolt stood and they strolled along the water's edge like Sunday peasants enjoying the sea after days of toil in the fields. They stopped near the shoreline where the boat was moored and watched the frenzied activity of the six busy sailors. Although Bolt gazed down at the long boat, his attention was focused on the rattling, clanking noises of the approaching wagon.

The wagon rolled to a jerky stop not more than thirty feet from where Bolt and Clarissa stood beside the open boat. He tugged the brim of his sombrero down so that a band of shade fell across his eyes. He glanced over at the two men who were climbing down from the driver's seat and saw Tom nod at him.

Bolt kept his head low enough for the band of shade to hide his eyes as he and Clarissa openly watched the unloading of the men from the back of the wagon. First to come through the canvas flap was a big muscled man bearing a rifle. He ordered the prisoners out and eight young men in rumpled clothing, their hands tied behind their backs, emerged from the hulk of the covered wagon.

Watley walked right past Bolt and Clarissa

when he went over to talk to the crew of the ship. The first man out of the wagon herded the prisoners toward the boat, nudging them with his rifle.

Pistol drawn, Tom walked over and stood next to Watley, his weapon trained on the prisoners. As the first bound man reached the edge of the boat and the loading of the prisoners began, Tom nodded to Bolt again. Bolt nodded back.

Tom raised his hand, then slammed the butt of his pistol against Watley's skull with a dull thud. Watley collapsed to the sandy ground, unconscious.

"Don't move," Tom ordered as he turned his pistol on the confused sailors.

Bolt and Clarissa moved in quickly with drawn weapons. Bolt smashed his pistol butt into the head of Watley's guard, knocking him out cold. As Clarissa trained her derringer on the sailors, Bolt brought out his knife and cut the thin rope that bound the hands of one of the prisoners. He handed the man the knife and told him to free the others. When they were free, they helped Bolt tie Watley's wrists together and load him into the boat.

"You're free to go home," Tom told the prisoners. "Take Watley's wagon."

"What about him?" one of the freed prisoners asked above the cheering of the others, as he pointed to the unconscious guard.

"Tie him up, hands and feet, and take him with

you. Dump him out when you get to a deserted stretch of road."

Bolt and Clarissa climbed into the boat and aimed their weapons at the crew members.

Tom was the last one to climb aboard.

"Pull anchor," he ordered. "We're ready to leave."

"Where you want us to take you?" asked one of the sailors who spoke English.

"Where were you supposed to take these men?" Tom asked.

"To Matamoros," said the sailor.

"Then take us there."


After more than a week in the water, the boat finally arrived at the coast of Matamoros, where another wagon, an open buckboard, was waiting for them. With a pistol in his back, Watley ordered the driver to take them to their final destination. Tom and Clarissa climbed in back and Bolt positioned Lyle Watley between the driver and himself.

Two armed guards greeted them when they arrived at the fenced-in hills where many men were at work, digging into the ground with picks and shovels, and carrying buckets back and forth.

"Tell my father I want to see him," Lyle Watley told the guards as Bolt shoved his out-of-sight pistol against Watley's ribs.

Bolt noticed the weathered sign at the entrance. BERTRAND WATLEY SILVER MINE.

Tom and Clarissa climbed down from the wagon and came around to the front.

"Slavery went out of fashion a few years back," Bolt told Lyle Watley as one of the guards walked to a nearby shack. "How much do you and your father pay Jessie Belle to supply you with your slaves? What's Jessie's connection."

"She's my sister," Watley said.

"Your sister? It all makes sense now. She opened that whorehouse just so you could lure men out there. Then you drug them and take them away in the middle of the night to a life of eternal slavery."

"You're figured it right," Watley said dryly.

"Pretty smart, kidnapping the drovers and drifters, who wouldn't be missed if they disappeared," Bolt said.

"We thought so," Lyle said.

"It might have worked, too, if you hadn't made one small mistake," Bolt said.

"What's that?" Watley turned and glared at Bolt.

"You kidnapped the wrong fellow. You see, Clarissa Mayfield happens to care very much about her brother who disappeared under mysterious circumstances."

"I thought you were supposed to be dead," Lyle said sarcastically.

"That's where you made another mistake. Thinking my friend Tom would actually kill me.

The loyalty of friends goes much deeper sometimes than the loyalty between blood relatives. But that's something you probably don't know about since you don't have any real friends. All of your acquaintances are dirty, corrupt bastards, just like you, and there ain't a trace of loyalty in them."

When white-haired Bertrand Watley arrived with the guard, Tom and Clarissa walked over and stood on either side of them and brought their pistols into view, aimed them at Bertrand's sides, chest high.

Bertrand's eyes widened with surprise. He started to say something.

"It's all over, Mister Watley," Bolt said. "Free your slaves or both you and your bastard son, Lyle, will die. And if you two die, it's over anyway because no more poor innocent men will be shipped down here. We've put a stop to that."

Bertrand started to go for his pistol.

Tom and Clarissa cocked the hammers of their weapons.

"It's over," Bolt said again. "Hand over your gun and then walk out there and tell your prisoners that they're free to go home."

Bertrand Watley looked up at his son and shook his head sadly. He eased the gun from his holster, handed it to Tom, then walked across the field, a broken man.

Within minutes, the prisoners started coming out of the mines and headed toward the freedom that awaited them on the other side of the fence.

"Randy!" Clarissa called out when she spotted her brother in the throng of men who came their way. Randy dashed into his sister's open arms and they both shed tears.

Bertrand Watley walked back to the wagon when he had spread the news that the men were free.

"Lyle," he said, "you can stay here and live with me. Maybe, if we start paying wages, we'll find enough men to help us work the mines. We won't make the fortune we wanted, but maybe we can make it work."

"Sorry to spoil your plans, Mister Watley," Bolt said, "but Lyle's going back with us. He's got to face the music back home. We're taking Lyle and Randy Mayfield and as many of the prisoners as we can carry."

Back at The Proud Peacock, Bolt and Tom delivered the cowering, sullen Lyle Watley to his sister, Jessie Belle. Randy Mayfield and six of the men who had been taken prisoner by Lyle were with Bolt.

Jessie's mouth fell open when she saw Bolt.

"I thought you were dead," she exclaimed.

"You thought wrong. You've got a choice, Jezebel, ma'am. You can leave The Proud Peacock, and Cow Town, and San Antonio for good. Or you can face charges from these men with me. And they're in an ugly mood."

"I'll leave," she said. "I didn't like running a whorehouse anyway."

"Goodbye, then," Bolt said. "It's been interesting to know you."

"Yeah, sure."

"You can say goodbye to me at my grave over at the Rocking Bar. I heard you didn't attend my burial services."

With that Bolt and his group left the house.

"What about those whores of Jessie's?" Tom asked as they walked toward their horses. "They've got no place to go, no jobs."

"Yeah," said Bolt. "We'll have to do something about that."

## WHITE SQUAW
### Zebra's Adult Western Series
by E. J. Hunter

| | |
|---|---|
| #1: SIOUX WILDFIRE | (1205, $2.50) |
| #2: BOOMTOWN BUST | (1286, $2.50) |
| #3: VIRGIN TERRITORY | (1314, $2.50) |
| #4: HOT TEXAS TAIL | (1359, $2.50) |
| #5: BUCKSKIN BOMBSHELL | (1410, $2.50) |
| #6: DAKOTA SQUEEZE | (1479, $2.50) |
| #10: SOLID AS A ROCK | (1831, $2.50) |
| #11: HOT-HANDED HEATHEN | (1882, $2.50) |
| #12: BALL AND CHAIN | (1930, $2.50) |
| #13: TRACK TRAMP | (1995, $2.50) |
| #14: RED TOP TRAMP | (2075, $2.50) |
| #15: HERE COMES THE BRIDE | (2174, $2.50) |

*Available wherever paperbacks are sold, or order direct from the Publisher. Send cover price plus 50¢ per copy for mailing and handling to Zebra Books, Dept. 2196, 475 Park Avenue South, New York, N.Y. 10016. Residents of New York, New Jersey and Pennsylvania must include sales tax. DO NOT SEND CASH.*

## SWEET MEDICINE'S PROPHECY
by Karen A. Bale

**#1: SUNDANCER'S PASSION**           (1778, $3.95)

Stalking Horse was the strongest and most desirable of the tribe, and Sun Dancer surrounded him with her spell-binding radiance. But the innocence of their love gave way to passion—and passion, to betrayal. Would their relationship ever survive the ultimate sin?

**#2: LITTLE FLOWER'S DESIRE**           (1779, $3.95)

Taken captive by savage Crows, Little Flower fell in love with the enemy, handsome brave Young Eagle. Though their hearts spoke what they could not say, they could only dream of what could never be. . . .

**#4: SAVAGE FURY**           (1768, $3.95)

Aeneva's rage knew no bounds when her handsome mate Trent commanded her to tend their tepee as he rode into danger. But under cover of night, she stole away to be with Trent and share whatever perils fate dealt them.

**#5: SUN DANCER'S LEGACY**           (1878, $3.95)

Aeneva's and Trenton's adopted daughter Anna becomes the light of their lives. As she grows into womanhood, she falls in love with blond Steven Randall. Together they discover the secrets of their passion, the bitterness of betrayal—and fight to fulfill the prophecy that is Anna's birthright.

# ASHES
## by William W. Johnstone

**OUT OF THE ASHES** (1137, $3.50)

Ben Raines hadn't looked forward to the War, but he knew it was coming. After the balloons went up, Ben was one of the survivors, fighting his way across the country, searching for his family, and leading a band of new pioneers attempting to bring American OUT OF THE ASHES.

**FIRE IN THE ASHES** (1310, $3.50)

It's 1999 and the world as we know it no longer exists. Ben Raines, leader of the Resistance, must regroup his rebels and prep them for bloody guerrilla war. But are they ready to face an even fiercer foe—the human mutants threatening to overpower the world!

**ANARCHY IN THE ASHES** (1387, $3.50)

Out of the smoldering nuclear wreckage of World War III, Ben Raines has emerged as the strong leader the Resistance needs. When Sam Hartline, the mercenary, joins forces with an invading army of Russians, Ben and his people raise a bloody banner of defiance to defend earth's last bastion of freedom.

**SMOKE FROM THE ASHES** (2191, $3.50)

Swarming across America's Southern tier march the avenging soldiers of Libyan blood terrorist Khamsin. Lurking in the blackened ruins of once-great cities are the mutant Night People, crazed killers of all who dare enter their domain. Only Ben Raines, his son Buddy, and a handful of Ben's Rebel Army remain to strike a blow for the survival of America and the future of the free world!

**ALONE IN THE ASHES** (1721, $3.50)

In this hellish new world there are human animals and Ben Raines—famed soldier and survival expert—soon becomes their hunted prey. He desperately tries to stay one step ahead of death, but no one can survive ALONE IN THE ASHES.

*Available wherever paperbacks are sold, or order direct from the Publisher. Send cover price plus 50¢ per copy for mailing and handling to Zebra Books, Dept. 2196, 475 Park Avenue South, New York, N.Y. 10016. Residents of New York, New Jersey and Pennsylvania must include sales tax. DO NOT SEND CASH.*

## THE SURVIVALIST SERIES
### by Jerry Ahern

| | |
|---|---|
| #1: TOTAL WAR | (0960, $2.50) |
| #2: THE NIGHTMARE BEGINS | (0810, $2.50) |
| #3: THE QUEST | (0851, $2.50) |
| #4: THE DOOMSAYER | (0893, $2.50) |
| #5: THE WEB | (1145, $2.50) |
| #6: THE SAVAGE HORDE | (1232, $2.50) |
| #7: THE PROPHET | (1339, $2.50) |
| #8: THE END IS COMING | (1374, $2.50) |
| #9: EARTH FIRE | (1405, $2.50) |
| #10: THE AWAKENING | (1478, $2.50) |
| #11: THE REPRISAL | (1590, $2.50) |
| #12: THE REBELLION | (1676, $2.50) |
| #13: PURSUIT | (1877, $2.50) |
| #14: THE TERROR | (1972, $2.50) |
| #15: OVERLORD | (2070, $2.50) |

## SHELTER
### by Paul Ledd

| | |
|---|---|
| #15: SAVAGE NIGHT | (1272, $2.25) |
| #16: WICHITA GUNMAN | (1299, $2.25) |
| #18: TABOO TERRITORY | (1379, $2.25) |
| #19: THE HARD MEN | (1428, $2.25) |
| #20: SADDLE TRAMP | (1465, $2.25) |
| #22: FAST-DRAW FILLY | (1612, $2.25) |
| #23: WANTED WOMAN | (1680, $2.25) |
| #24: TONGUE-TIED TEXAN | (1794, $2.25) |
| #25: THE SLAVE QUEEN | (1869, $2.25) |
| #26: TREASURE CHEST | (1955, $2.25) |
| #27: HEAVENLY HANDS | (2023, $2.25) |
| #28: LAY OF THE LAND | (2148, $2.50) |